JENNA ST. JAMES

Cheryl,
Enjoy!
Jenna!

JENNA ST. JAMES BOOKS

Ryli Sinclair Mystery Series Order

Picture Perfect Murder
Girls' Night Out Murder
Old-Fashioned Murder
Bed, Breakfast, and Murder
Veiled in Murder
Bachelorettes and Bodies
Rings, Veils, and Murder
Last Stop Murder

Sullivan Sisters Mystery Series Order

Murder on the Vine
Burning Hot Murder
Prepear to Die

DEDICATION

This book is dedicated to all of my readers that enjoy the crazy antics of Aunt Shirley and Ryli. I've loved writing this series...watching the characters evolve and change over time. I hope you have, too. Thank you, readers, for taking this journey with me.

CHAPTER 1

"I can't believe I have to go," I whined to my best friend, Paige. "You and the twins just got out of the hospital yesterday. I haven't had enough time with you guys."

Paige laughed and finished changing a diaper. "You came to see us every day in the hospital. You didn't miss out on anything, Ryli. And you won't miss out on anything the four days you'll be gone. Besides, I'll text you pictures hourly."

"You better!"

Paige thrust a swaddled baby at me and I took it willingly. Unfortunately, I had no idea which one I took.

"Which one is this?" I asked.

Paige looked down at the baby in her arms. "I have Olivia, so you have Peyton."

"How do you do that?" I asked. "They just look like tiny wrinkled babies to me."

Paige shrugged. "I just know. There are slight differences between the two girls."

My brother, Matt, and sister-in-law, Paige, had delivered healthy twin girls last Saturday…the night of my wedding. Well, technically the twins weren't born until Sunday morning, but they sure put the final hoorah on the wedding reception. Lucky for us, nearly every EMT Granville employs was at the wedding reception, so getting Paige to the hospital was a piece of cake—pun intended.

Mom had had the presence of mind to grab the middle section of the cake and take it with her. So we all celebrated by pacing and eating wedding cake in the waiting room.

4

"Lasagna is made," Mom said as she strode into Paige's living room. "All you have to do is heat it up."

"Thanks, Janine," Paige said. "I don't know what I'd do if it weren't for you and my mom. You guys are a blessing."

Mom reached down and took Olivia from Paige. "That's what grandmothers do." Mom walked over to the recliner and cooed over her twin.

"Thanks for keeping Miss Molly while Garrett and I are away," I said to Mom.

She smiled and kissed the top of Olivia's head. "Well, I have to take care of my fur grandbaby, too."

"Are you packed?" Paige asked.

I rolled my eyes. "Yes. I'm going to go pick up Aunt Shirley and Old Man Jenkins around noon, then head over to the police station to pick up Garrett. He's leaving his vehicle there."

My hunky new husband is the Chief of Police for the citizens of Granville, Missouri…population ten thousand. Neither one of us had planned on going on a honeymoon immediately after we were married. We wanted to wait and go when the time was right. Unfortunately, Aunt Shirley jumped the gun and bought honeymoon tickets not only for her and Old Man Jenkins, but for Garrett and me, too.

"Seems to me everything's ready," Paige snickered. "No reason you can't go off and have a great time on your honeymoon…with Aunt Shirley in tow."

"It's a good thing I'm holding my niece right now," I grumbled, "or I'd lay you flat out on the floor."

"Ryli Jo!" Mom scolded lightly.

Paige laughed as she pushed herself up from the couch and lumbered over to a large basket. "I guess this laundry over here isn't going to fold itself." She scooted the basket over to the couch and started folding tiny clothes, socks, and blankets. "I swear, every time I turn around, three more loads of baby things need to be washed."

Mom and I chuckled over Paige's lament.

"Now, Ryli, you and Garrett make sure you take moments to be alone and just spend time together," Mom said. "Don't let Aunt Shirley dominate your whole trip. The only comfort I have is knowing there's virtually no trouble you two can get into. You'll be on a moving train, you can't really get off for long periods of time, you won't have weapons, and there's no place for you two to run around and get in trouble."

I would totally be offended if Mom wasn't right. Aunt Shirley and I did have a pretty high track record when it came to finding dead bodies and then having to solve murders. But this time, Mom had nothing to worry about. There was no way I was going to let Aunt Shirley rope me into doing anything ridiculous on my honeymoon.

Or so I told myself.

***

"I should have known you'd pack the whole world." I heaved the last of Aunt Shirley's suitcases into the trunk of the Falcon and slammed the lid closed. "We're gonna be gone four days, not four weeks."

6

"Hush," Aunt Shirley said. "You know I have to make sure I have an outfit for every occasion."

"I'm staying out of this," Old Man Jenkins said as he and Aunt Shirley got in the backseat. "She's already yelled at me ten times this morning."

Aunt Shirley scoffed. "Oh, I have not. And it's not yelling. It's simply me reminding you of all the things you've done wrong today."

I met Old Man Jenkins's eyes in the rearview mirror, and he gave his a small roll for me. I smiled and said nothing as I pulled out of the Manor—the assisted living facility where Aunt Shirley and Old Man Jenkins lived.

"I texted Garrett before I picked you up," I said. "I told him we'd be at the station shortly to get him."

"Is he excited?" Aunt Shirley asked. "I bet he is. Four days of honeymoon relaxation."

Four days on a train with you, Aunt Shirley...don't bet on it.

"Well, he's packed if that means anything." I didn't have the heart to tell her the truth about how Garrett was really feeling about this double honeymoon trip.

It only takes about five minutes to get anywhere in Granville. The town is made up of two main streets, numerous businesses on the square, and all the other fixings in a small town...schools, houses, and churches. Not much has changed in the thirty years I've lived here.

Garrett was standing outside waiting on me as I pulled into the Granville Police Department parking lot. He was scowling as he opened the door...but seeing as how Garrett was usually scowling around Aunt Shirley, I didn't take it to heart.

"Well, Ace, you ready to party?" Aunt Shirley asked from the backseat.

I saw Garrett bristle at the nickname.

"Don't worry," I whispered. "We'll drink a lot and never leave our sleeping car."

Garrett's mouth curved upward in a smile. "Count on it, Sin."

I shivered at the prospect of four uninterrupted days with my new husband. No one calling him into work. No one—namely me—stumbling over a dead body. No one chasing bad guys—that could be either Garrett *or* me.

Just the two of us, on a train, free drinks, our own sleeping car, and all the alone time we wanted. Suddenly, this trip didn't seem so bad.

CHAPTER 2

"That was the worst security I've ever seen," Aunt Shirley grumbled as she plopped down in a seat at the terminal. "I bet I could have at least smuggled my nunchucks in my suitcase!"

"And for the tenth time now," Garrett said impatiently, "you don't need any weapons. It's your honeymoon, or have you forgotten?"

"I ain't forgotten, Ace," Aunt Shirley grinned wickedly. "Why do you think I packed my leather pants and riding crop?"

"Shirley Jenkins," Old Man Jenkins warned, "no one wants to hear this."

Aunt Shirley barreled on as if Old Man Jenkins never spoke. "Or the white nightie with the see-through top part here." Aunt Shirley lifted both her hands and waved them over her sagging chest. "Or the fact that I packed whipped cream in our ice chest."

"I'd give anything for the zombie apocalypse to start right now," Garrett deadpanned.

I giggled but understood where he was coming from. It had taken me a long time to get used to Aunt Shirley's antics. Nowadays, her outlandish words hardly affected me at all.

"We should be boarding in about twenty minutes," I said. "I've been reading the brochure, and this should actually be fun. I guess it's something new the railroad company has started. See." I leaned over and showed Garrett the brochure. "Since we are doing a western theme, the inside of our train should be done in a lot of woods and old-style train details."

"That's cool," Garrett said. "What's that one?"

He'd pointed to the Southern Plantation package. "That one starts in Little Rock, Arkansas then drops down and goes all through Louisiana. The train even stops overnight so riders can tour a haunted plantation and other scary things. Then it goes up through Mississippi and over to Little Rock, again. The outside of the train is done in the old traditional black, as is much of the inside." I turned the page in the brochure and pointed to the dining car. "It's mostly done in black and dark blues with splashes of white throughout. Creepy, don't you think?"

"Sure is," Garrett agreed. "You like this kind of stuff, don't you?"

I felt my face flush. "Yeah. I love the idea of themed vacations. And these seem pretty cool."

"I actually did some research before I bought these tickets," Aunt Shirley said to Garrett. "I chose the Westward Expansion package because I thought it would be the most enjoyable for you and the old man."

Garrett looked contrite. "I apologize, Aunt Shirley, if I've made you think I don't appreciate this. I do. It's just a little unorthodox going on a honeymoon with your immediate family."

Old Man Jenkins nodded vigorously, but Aunt Shirley ignored him. "Maybe we'll be trendsetters when the other people on the train find out!"

I didn't think the others would be impressed, but I didn't want to hurt Aunt Shirley's feelings.

"I'd say these vacations are catching on," I said. "There's probably thirty people here."

A loud cracking sound reverberated overhead, and a pleasant voice came over the loud speaker. "Ladies and gentlemen, we will begin boarding the Westward Expansion shortly. Please look at your tickets. If you are riding in our luxury cabins, you will see the letter A, B, C, or D assigned to your ticket. Once you find your letter, you will see overhead signs in our terminal with your letter. Go ahead and make your way over to the appropriate letter. If you are riding coach, you can make your way to the center aisle."

Garrett stood and lifted the handle of our wheeled suitcase. "Looks like we're in D."

"Oh, I'm so excited!" Aunt Shirley squealed as the four of us strolled over to aisle D.

I had to admit, I was pretty excited myself.

A tall, thin man in his early forties dressed in a traditional porter uniform waved us over. Next to him, an older, petite bald man also dressed in a porter uniform stood unsmiling as he ran his gaze over us. I judged him to be around mid to late fifties. There were six other passengers in line waiting for instructions.

A husband and wife team, sporting matching wedding bands, looked to be in their forties. He was of average height, build, and looks. Nothing really stood out about him to me. His wife, on the other hand, oozed femininity. Her dark brown hair was pulled back in a fancy updo, and her black pantsuit reeked of money. The hostile looks they were shooting each other had me wondering about their current relationship.

Another couple off to the side looked totally out of place. He was a large man with an even larger receding hairline. His complexion was ruddy, his cheeks sagged nearly to his jawline, and his nose was bulbous and red. He was reading the riot act to the mousy woman with him. She was his complete opposite. Her blonde-brown hair was pulled back in a knot at her neck, her shoulders looked to be in a permanent hunch, and her body was reed thin. The sunken eyes and set line of her thin lips portrayed a woman unhappy with her life.

Another man who looked to be traveling alone was busy scrolling through his phone. I put him around sixty. I couldn't see the color of his hair because of the black cowboy hat he wore, but his shoulders were broad, as was the rest of him. Even though he was an older man, I could tell by his physique he spent a lot of hours working outside. He had dark eyes, a prominent nose, and a nicely sculpted jawline.

There was one other person in our group, a well-dressed woman in her mid-seventies. Her short, silver hair was perfectly coiffed, and she looked chic in a white turtleneck/sweater combo paired with black, wide-legged pants. In her arms was a long-haired Maltese with a matching blue bow and blue collar set.

"Your dog is beautiful," I said.

She smiled gratefully at me. "Thank you, dear. I just love my little Muffy. She goes everywhere with me."

"Why did nearly everyone line up either in this aisle or coach?" Aunt Shirley asked. "If there are three other sections available, why aren't we over there?"

The older lady ran her wrinkled hand down Muffy's back soothingly. "Because there are three other major stops on this tour and those people will go in one of those sleeping cars." She paused and rubbed her cheek against Muffy's neck. "My name's Eloise Rothchild, and this is my fourth time taking this tour. I usually ride about every three months or so."

"Must be a pretty spectacular tour," Old Man Jenkins said.

"Oh, it is. The workers are wonderful, and Muffy loves the view."

I bit my cheek to keep from laughing. Mainly because I knew she wasn't joking. She obviously adored Muffy, and if she thought Muffy wanted to take this trip every three months, then she'd make sure Muffy was on the train.

The tall porter clapped his hands together to get everyone's attention. "Ladies and gentlemen, let me be the first to welcome you aboard the Westward Expansion. My name is Christopher, and this here," he pointed to the petite man next to him, "is Delbert, and we're here to make your stay with us as pleasant as possible." His deep-set blue eyes twinkled and his blonde handlebar mustache moved up and down as he spoke. "I personally believe you are the luckiest bunch because your sleeping cars are the closest to the dining hall."

I chuckled at his joke.

"In a few moments we will begin loading the train. Please follow Delbert and me down the platform and onto the train. It may be a little loud at first, but that's just the hustle and bustle of getting a train up and going." Christopher pushed open the door and hurried outside. "Follow me, please."

"This is it," Garrett murmured. "No going back now."

I giggled but gave him a stern glare. He lifted his shoulder as if to ask me why I was angry.

"Hurry," Aunt Shirley hissed. "We're already falling behind."

I rolled my eyes and practically stepped on Mrs. Rothchild's heels as I ran to catch up.

Loud was an understatement.

There were so many hisses, pops, and whistles I thought my ears were going to burst. I stopped behind Mrs. Rothchild and willed her to hurry up the steps so my ears would stop bleeding. Just when I thought my head would explode, Christopher leaned down and wrapped his hands around Mrs. Rothchild's upper arms and expertly lifted her up the step and onto the train. I was tempted to help, but the only thing I could really do was give her a push on her backside...which in turn would probably give the elderly woman a heart attack. When the space was empty, I hopped up onto the train and continued following Mrs. Rothchild and Christopher down a long corridor, noticing a set of tiny stairs immediately to my left.

Christopher and Delbert stopped at a doorway but motioned me to continue following Mrs. Rothchild. I looked back and noticed that Delbert had not stopped watching Mrs. Rothchild. When we were all squeezed into the long, narrow passageway, Christopher spoke up.

"I will try and make this as quick as possible so everyone can get settled in. The bottom here is where you all will be sleeping. All rooms have a queen bed, two chairs, a room-length window, your own personal bathroom, and a mini-fridge to hold whatever food and drinks you brought with you."

"Wow," I whispered to Garrett. "I had no idea these cabins were that nice."

"We try and give everyone as much privacy as possible, but still maintain order. Breakfast is served in the dining car from seven until ten. The dining car is closed for lunch, but there is a fully-stocked lounge that sells sandwiches, chips, and drinks of all sorts, both alcoholic and non-alcoholic. Then dinner will be served in the dining car from five to seven. Due to the number of people on the train, we need to make sure we have a steady flow, so you all are assigned dining car one. Please be sure to sit in your assigned section so as not to break up any other groups on the train. The dining cars are marked at each door entrance, so there should be no problem knowing which car is yours."

"It's very easy to find," Mrs. Rothchild added.

"Again, my name is Christopher and this is Delbert. Delbert will help get you unpacked and settled in your cabins. I will be your porter, steward, whatever you want to call me for the duration of your stay on the Westward Expansion. I also have a sleeping car down here, so if you need anything at any time, just ring for me. You each will be given a key for your door, so don't worry about having to leave your personal items unattended. And while we do have a person on the train in charge of security, I don't foresee a problem. We've never had a theft before."

Christopher motioned to the set of stairs on his left. "If you follow these stairs, it will lead you to the main portion of the train. Each section of the train—you all being in section D—has their own panoramic viewing car and lounge. So again, you will have some privacy from the other passengers. Once you ascend the stairs you will be in the viewing car. If you follow it on out to the right, you will be in the lounge, and one more car over will be the beginning of the dining hall. Immediately to your left when you ascend the stairs is a set of doors and a small walkway that will lead you to the coach area of the train."

"Where do those people get their drinks?" the large man with the ruddy complexion demanded.

Christopher frowned. "They are free to eat and drink wherever."

"So not total privacy?" the large man taunted.

Christopher ignored the question and looked down at his clipboard. "I will be in the first sleeping car here by the staircase in case you need me. The next cabin is Mrs. Rothchild's, then I have Harold and Angelica Walsh, followed by Garrett and Ryli Kimble, then Waylon and Shirley Jenkins, Floyd and June Hughes, and finally Clive Salter."

There was an awkward dance as we all shuffled around each other so that everyone could get to their sleeping cars.

"Excuse me, dears," Mrs. Rothchild said as she and Muffy slowly squeezed their way around Garrett, Aunt Shirley, Old Man Jenkins, and me. "I always have this cabin next to Christopher's. So he can keep an eye on me."

The old lady pushed open her door and Christopher handed her a key. "I'll check on you in a moment, madam."

"No rush, Christopher."

Mrs. Rothchild closed and locked the door.

"Why does she get Christopher to help her unpack," the same large rude man grumbled, "and we get the little guy who doesn't look like he could lift a suitcase."

I glanced over at Delbert to see if he'd heard the inconsiderate man. If Delbert had, he didn't indicate he had. In fact, Delbert seemed intent on watching Mrs. Rothchild's closed door.

"I can get into our room now," I said. "That should clear up some space."

I opened the door assigned to us and walked into the cabin.

16

"Oh my," I whispered. "This is way better than I thought possible."

"It *is* nice," Garrett agreed as he rolled our suitcase against the wall under the window.

The interior walls of the car were done in a mahogany wood finish, and the polish from the hardwood floor gleamed bright. I wasn't sure what kind of bulbs they were using, but the antique lights flickered like they were gas-lit lights from long ago. I opened the only door in the room and took in the white pedestal sink, toilet, and corner shower stall. I walked over to the toilet and frowned. There was something odd about it.

It took me a few more seconds before I realized it didn't have a handle.

Stepping back I looked all around the toilet and realized there was a lever in front of the toilet you could step on. I gingerly stepped on it and the bottom of the toilet slid open, and a loud suction noise emitted from the toilet as water rushed in from all sides. I quickly stepped off the lever and the bottom slid closed again. It was set up like a toilet on an airplane.

"This toilet's a little hinky. And scary."

Garrett chuckled. "I did a couple tours overseas. I'm used to hinky bathrooms. In fact, it's more than what I had at times."

I shuddered at the thought of not having a proper bathroom.

"We'll manage," Garrett assured me.

"I suppose." I walked back into the sleeping car and grinned saucily at my new husband. "We have a couple hours until supper. What should we do?"

"Well, Mrs. Kimble, I have a couple suggestions in mind."

A knock at the door interrupted our mood. I was about to give Aunt Shirley a piece of my mind as I flung the door open, but instead of Aunt Shirley, it was the petite porter, Delbert.

"Sorry to bother you," Delbert said, pointing to the suitcase still on the bed, "but it's my job to help you unpack and get you anything you may need."

I blinked in surprise. I really wasn't wanting someone else pawing through my things...especially since I had a lot of honeymoon clothing with me.

"We should be okay, Delbert," Garrett said smoothly. "But I bet the couple next door could use your help. The older woman, Shirley, is pretty old and feeble. She knows it, so it's okay to say you'd like to help her because she's old and feeble."

Delbert nodded sagely. "Of course. I'll go right now and see to her."

I couldn't help the grin that spread across my face. Garrett was definitely going to get an earful later.

CHAPTER 3

"It's about time you two were coming up for air." Aunt Shirley reclined against the arm of an ornate, antique chaise in the lounge and sipped on a glass of champagne.

"We're on our honeymoon," I said. "You're lucky we're coming out of the cabin at all."

Aunt Shirley snorted. "Technically we're on *our* honeymoon too, and you don't see me acting the fool."

"Night's still young," Garrett quipped.

Old Man Jenkins laughed and slapped Garrett on the back. "Good one, son."

Aunt Shirley opened her mouth, but I jumped in to smooth things over. "Going fancy on me?" I joked as I pointed to her glass of champagne.

Usually Aunt Shirley's drink of choice was tequila. Or as I liked to think of it…to-kill-ya.

"Fancy times call for fancy swill," Aunt Shirley quipped. "And our handsome bartender, Jack, said it was a good champagne." She took another sip. "He was right."

"I'm having a bourbon that was aged twenty years in a barrel," Old Man Jenkins said excitedly. "How about having a glass with me?"

"Sounds great," Garrett said.

"Go ahead and order me some champagne," I said. "Good thing I wore my fancy dress."

Garrett grinned and whispered in my ear.

"Stop whispering naughty things in her ear," Aunt Shirley demanded. "Go have a drink with my old man and leave us newlywed girls alone. I haven't had a moment to myself since we got on the train. Right after we got in the room, that short little guy, Delbert, came by to help me unpack. He said he heard I was old and feeble and may need help unpacking. Talk about rude!"

I bit my lip to keep from laughing as I sat down next to Aunt Shirley. A few seconds later Garrett handed me a glass of champagne before returning to the bar. Both of our men were leaning back against the bar's countertop, surveying the room.

The weather-beaten, older man I saw earlier from our group wearing the black cowboy hat ambled into the lounge. He was even more ruggedly handsome up close.

"Evenin', ladies." He put his hand on his hat and tipped it slightly at Aunt Shirley and me. "You two are looking lovely tonight."

Aren't you a smooth one.

Aunt Shirley tittered. "Thank you, sir. So nice of you to say."

I rolled my eyes at Garrett...he grinned and sipped his bourbon.

"You can call me Clive. Clive Salter to be exact."

Aunt Shirley batted her lashes at Clive. "My name is Shirley, and this here is my niece, Ryli. Up at the bar are our men."

Clive's eyes cut to Old Man Jenkins and Garrett. "I think I'll join you fellas for a drink, if that's okay with you?"

"Sure thing," Old Man Jenkins said.

The lounge doors opened again.

"I don't care what you say," an angry voice said, "that little guy had no right to go through my things."

"Floyd," his mousy wife whispered, "please don't cause a scene."

Floyd whirled around and leaned down into his wife's face. "I'll do whatever I darn well please. Don't you ever tell me how to act."

The mousy woman wrung her hangs together. "I'm sorry. I just thought—"

"Well don't. No one cares to hear what you're thinking."

She stumbled back as though she'd been slapped. "Of course. I'm sorry, Floyd."

Floyd whirled back around and strode to the bar. "Give me a shot of whiskey."

Mousy winced and barely lifted her eyes off the floor as she searched for a place to sit.

I had a feeling this wasn't Floyd's first whiskey of the night.

Aunt Shirley glared at Floyd as he bellied up to the bar next to Old Man Jenkins.

"Times like these," Aunt Shirley whispered, "I wish I'd brought my nunchucks. Nice hit upside the head would make him think twice."

I nodded my head sagely. "Or you could just shoot him."

Floyd's wife inhaled sharply. I could tell she'd heard me. Feeling my face heat up, I tried to come up with a quick excuse as to why I would trash her husband...but I had nothing.

"Do you mind if I sit here?" Mousy indicated to an empty chair across from us against the wall.

"No," I said quickly. "Have a seat. I couldn't help but overhear as you came through the door. Was your husband talking about Delbert?"

Mousy nodded her head. "I think it's part of the service. The man just wanted to help us unpack. He said it was part of his job. It's just Floyd doesn't like people going through his things."

Mousy said the last part in a panicked whisper.

I nodded my head. "Yes, that's part of Delbert's job. He came to our room, too. My name's Ryli Sincl—I mean, Ryli Kimble. I just got married last week, so I'm still getting used to the name."

Mousy smiled shyly. "Newlyweds. That's lovely."

"Thanks. Anyway, I'm Ryli Kimble and this is Aunt Shirley. Aunt Shirley also just got married for the first time about a month ago."

Mousy's eyes bulged. "Really? Wow. That's...unusual."

Aunt Shirley waved her glass in the air. "And I hadn't planned on getting married this time, either. But the old goat went and tricked me into it. Got me drunk in Vegas and the next morning I woke up...married!"

"Well now, if that don't beat all," Clive said from the bar. "Congratulations." He tipped his drink to Old Man Jenkins before taking a huge gulp.

Mousy blinked rapidly. "Well, I hope you two are happy."

Aunt Shirley shrugged. "I ain't *unhappy,* so I guess it's okay."

"What about you?" I asked. "What's your name?"

I didn't want to have to call her Mousy the next three days.

"Oh, sorry. My name's June Hughes, and that's my husband, Floyd, over there." She pointed to the loudmouth at the bar.

"Are you just on vacation?" I asked. "Or are you traveling to see someone?"

22

"Actually, I won this trip last month in a raffle," June said. "The grocery store I always shop at was having a raffle-off, and it didn't cost anything to enter. I couldn't believe it when the store called me and said I'd won. I'd never won anything ever before!"

Floyd continued to glare at June as he tossed back his whiskey. "Give me another shot." Floyd turned back to the bar and slammed his glass down.

June looked down at her hands folded in her lap.

No way was I going to be able to handle this for three more days. I gave Garrett the stink eye, hoping he'd step in.

Aunt Shirley winked at me. "You know I recently read that if a man has more than one drink of hard liquor a night, he's unable to perform in the sack. Seems his," Aunt Shirley let out a whistle and simultaneously pointed her finger downward, "is unable to rise to the occasion. Good thing my old man doesn't drink excessively."

Garrett, Old Man Jenkins, and Clive laughed out loud.

Floyd turned around and glared at Aunt Shirley. "You got an awful big mouth on you for an old lady."

Oh…he'd gone and done it now.

I looked at Old Man Jenkins and Garrett. Both men seemed to be enjoying the show.

Fortunately—or unfortunately, depending on how you look at it—Aunt Shirley was saved from beating Floyd to death when Mrs. Rothchild glided elegantly through the door and into the lounge. Her formal, midnight-blue rhinestoned dress glittered in the light. Muffy had on her matching blue bow and blue rhinestoned collar.

"I hope I'm not late," Mrs. Rothchild said. "I fell asleep the minute the train took off. An unfortunate hazard when you get to be my age."

I stood and offered her my seat next to Aunt Shirley. "Mrs. Rothchild, why don't you and Muffy sit here. I need a refill on my glass of champagne anyway. Can I get you a glass?"

"Aren't you just the sweetest girl. That would be lovely." Mrs. Rothchild plopped down next to Aunt Shirley and stroked Muffy's fur. "I saw the four of you sitting together in the station. Are you guys together?"

"Sure are," Aunt Shirley said. "We are honeymooning together!"

Mrs. Rothchild blinked. "Come again?"

"Ryli is my great-niece. She and Garrett just got married last week. And that old man standing up at the bar is now my husband as of three weeks ago."

Mrs. Rothchild nodded. "If that don't beat all. Congratulations to each of you."

I slipped my arm through Garrett's and rested my head against his shoulder. He grabbed my glass and half-turned to hand the glass to our bartender Jack. "Two more please."

Jack smiled and nodded at me. "Sure thing."

"How much longer until dinner is served?" Floyd grumbled. "It's ridiculous we have to wait until a certain time to eat."

"Should only be a matter of minutes, sir." Jack handed me my drinks with another smile but spoke to Floyd.

"I think we're still missing one more couple," Mrs. Rothchild said.

I walked the short span to Mrs. Rothchild and handed her a glass of champagne before returning to Garrett's side.

A few seconds later the last couple in our party entered. It was the average looking guy with the knockout wife. He was impeccably dressed in a dark suit and red power tie. His black shoes were as slick and shiny as his black hair, and his eyes looked like he bore the weight of a thousand pounds. His wife had changed from her black pantsuit into a gray, short-sleeved, body-hugging dress that fell to her feet. Her earrings, dinner rings, and bracelet all matched. I had to admit, I was pretty jealous of how poised this woman managed to look.

"Good evening," the man said. "My name is Harold Walsh, and this is my wife, Angelica."

We all greeted them—except for Floyd. He was still too busy glaring at everyone.

"Do you want something to drink?" Harold Walsh asked his wife.

Angelica's eyes cut to the champagne in my hand, and her mouth curled up in a small sneer. "I'll have a glass of red wine."

I half expected claws to pop out of her fingertips.

Jack was pouring more drinks when the lights suddenly dimmed then came back on.

"Looks like dinner is ready to be served," Jack said. "You guys should go on ahead. The other passengers will start making their way back here to the dining car in a few seconds."

He didn't have to tell me twice. I pushed myself off the bar and started toward our dining car.

CHAPTER 4

"Come and sit," Christopher motioned to me. "I assume you four want to dine together?"

"Thank you." I slid against the wall of the train while the others followed behind me.

"We want a table alone," Floyd said. "We'll take that one." He'd pointed to the only other four-person table available in the dining car.

Christopher looked down his nose at Floyd. "That one has already been reserved."

"Who says?" Floyd demanded.

Christopher stood a little taller. "Mrs. Rothchild always asks to dine in a four-person table so she can mingle with the other guests."

"What makes her so special?" Floyd grumbled.

Before the situation got totally out of control, Clive spoke up. "Well, I don't mind dining with the little lady. That is, if you'll allow me to sit with you?"

Mrs. Rothchild blushed and nuzzled Muffy's head. "I'd like that Mr. Salter."

"Call me Clive," he said as he squeezed his way around Floyd and his wife.

"I guess that leaves the Hughes at this two person," Christopher said as he pointed to the table next to Rothchild and Salter, "and the Walshes can sit here." He pointed to the table across from us.

26

I rolled my eyes at Aunt Shirley as Floyd grumbled and whined about the unfairness. This guy was definitely making the trip a drag.

Christopher handed each of us a paper menu with about ten different dinners to choose from. As I read over the meals, my stomach growled.

I heard voices behind me and turned to watch through the narrow opening as other passengers sat down in the dining car behind us. "They must be the passengers in sleeping car C bound for Denver."

"What time do we get into Denver again?" Aunt Shirley asked.

"Eight in the morning," Harold Walsh answered.

We all looked at Harold and he smoothed down his tie. "Sorry. Couldn't help but overhear the question. I just know we arrive at eight because I have an appointment at eight-thirty around the corner from the train station."

"What kind of appointment?" Aunt Shirley asked.

Harold's face turned pink and his eyes cut to his wife's. "Just a little business endeavor."

Angelica Walsh's lips thinned and she narrowed her eyes at her husband. "Which you better hope goes well."

Harold cleared his throat. "Yes. Which I hope goes well." He reached down and picked up his drink and took a large swallow.

I raised my eyebrows at Aunt Shirley.

It was like everyone was either super creepy or super cryptic on this train.

Delbert ambled over and set four waters in front of us before informing us that Christopher would be around shortly to take our dinner orders. He moved quickly to the next table and set down their drinks.

"Is there anything else I can get for you, Mrs. Rothchild?" Delbert asked.

"No, thank you." Mrs. Rothchild picked up her water glass and took a little sip. "It's perfect, Delbert."

Delbert frowned. "Very well."

Christopher suddenly appeared at my elbow and took our order. I settled on the blackened chicken since Garrett ordered the steak. I figured I could sneak bites off his plate and sample both the chicken and steak. Married life definitely had its perks!

"So what's on the agenda after dinner?" I asked. "Not like we can actually go someplace."

Aunt Shirley clapped her hands together. "I thought the four of us might play some poker in the lounge. We haven't done that in a while."

Old Man Jenkins smiled at Aunt Shirley. "If memory serves, the last time we played poker together you nearly got banned from the Manor."

Aunt Shirley snorted. "Those sticks in the mud. You have one little strip poker party and the whole place comes down on you!"

Clive and Mrs. Rothchild laughed. Clive turned sideways in his seat and leaned against the train wall. "That must have been some party, huh?"

Old Man Jenkins looked at Aunt Shirley then back at Clive. "Sure was. That was pretty much the night I knew I had to have this woman. Of course, it took nearly eight more months before she finally said I do."

28

Aunt Shirley narrowed her eyes. "I wouldn't exactly say I jumped at the chance of marriage."

"I like that," Clive said. "Reminds me of my marriage and my wife…God rest her soul."

My heart lurched. "You're a widower? I'm sorry."

"Yes," Mrs. Rothchild said as she put Muffy in her oversized purse. "I'm sorry to hear that."

Clive's eyes misted over. "Been about a year now."

"Is that why you're taking this trip?" Mrs. Rothchild asked. "Just to get away for a while?"

Clive squirmed in his seat a bit—an odd sight for such a large man. "Not exactly. I have a pretty big farm in northern Missouri, but it's too much for me now. My son has moved to Kansas City and wants no part in helping me run the farm, and I'm getting too old to run it myself." He took a small sip from his glass before continuing. "Plus, my Anna had cancer, and the bills have pretty much wiped me out. I have to start selling off my livestock. I contacted a friend of mine down by Oklahoma City. He has a big spread down there and is interested in buying my cows." Clive chuckled wryly and surreptitiously wiped his eye. "And then I thought what the heck. Might as well enjoy the trip. So I booked this train excursion. Who knows…this might be the last grand adventure I go on for a while."

"I'm sorry about your wife," I said and squeezed Garrett's hand.

Clive dipped his head toward me. "Thank you, little lady. I appreciate that. My Anna was an amazing woman. She didn't deserve to go the way she did."

Garrett leaned down and kissed my cheek. "I love you."

Christopher arrived with our dinner and conversations stopped while we dug in.

"That's me!" Aunt Shirley suddenly announced part-way through the meal as she yanked her cell phone out of her bra. She scrolled through the messages, letting Old Man Jenkins look over her shoulder, before passing the phone to me. "You'll love these pictures."

I gingerly took the phone—after all, it had been where no person or thing should ever have to go. Aunt Shirley's favorite spot to keep things besides her oversized purse. Paige had sent a group text of what the twins had done that day. There were countless pictures of the two girls screaming and crying, countless diaper changes, countless feeding sessions…and the very last picture was of the twins sleeping.

"Those were great." I handed Aunt Shirley back her cell phone. "Poor Paige is going to go insane before they even turn a month old."

"Where's your phone?" Aunt Shirley demanded.

"I left it in the sleeping car. I didn't think I'd have a need for it."

I finished off the last of the delicious dinner and poured another glass of champagne from the bottle on our table.

"Dessert tonight," Christopher said once the dishes were removed, "consists of either tiramisu or double-chocolate cake with fudge icing."

I moaned. "I'm gonna have to wear leggings this whole trip! I'll never be able to button my jeans at this rate."

"What can I get for you folks?" Christopher asked.

"I'll take the tiramisu, and Ryli will have the cake," Garrett said. "This way she can eat both."

"God I love you," I whispered.

As I was preparing a space to put my desserts, Muffy let out a string of cute little doggie sneezes. When she was finished, she flung her head as if to clear it. And off flew her dog collar, landing at June Hughes's feet.

"Oops." June bent down to pick up the dog collar. "I think Muffy dropped this."

"Oh my!" Mrs. Rothchild cried. "Thank you so much. I've been meaning to get the clasp fixed. It was silly of me to get such a simple clasp. I should have had the jeweler make it buckle like a normal collar, but I thought the delicate clasp looked daintier for my Muffy."

"I'm sure it's an easy fix," Clive said. "Wait, did you say you had a *jeweler* make the dog collar?"

All eyes turned to Mrs. Rothchild. "Why yes. I can't have my Muffy wearing just any old collar. This one here was made special for her birthday last year. It matches my dress. There are six pink diamonds around the blue collar, each one a carat."

No one said a word. I swear you could hear a pin drop in our dining car.

"What did something like that cost?" Angelica Walsh asked.

"Angelica!" Harold hissed. "You can't ask a question like that."

Angelica shrugged. "I'm just curious."

Only she didn't look just curious…she looked like she was adding up the figures in her head and formulating a plan.

Mrs. Rothchild waved her hand in the air. "It's okay. About thirty thousand for the stones, and another five thousand to actually have the collar made to my specifications."

CHAPTER 5

Clive let out a whistle. "That's a nice chunk of change."

"You spent thirty-five *thousand* dollars on a *dog* collar?" Floyd scoffed. "You obviously have more money than brains."

June sucked in her breath. "Floyd!"

Floyd scowled at his wife. "Who spends that kind of money on a *mutt*?"

Mrs. Rothchild lifted her chin in the air and put her hands over Muffy's ears. "Muffy is *not* a mutt. Both of her parents were purebred Maltese dogs. And, besides, the dog collar is insured."

"It's still thirty-five thousand dollars on a *dog*," Floyd grumbled.

Clive frowned. "And I'd argue it's her money to do with as she pleases."

Angelica grabbed her wine glass off the table. "Well, it would *please me* if she gave me some of that money."

"That's enough," Harold warned his wife.

Angelica rolled her eyes at Harold and sipped at her wine.

I gave Aunt Shirley a pointed look but didn't say anything.

"I'll admit, thirty-five thousand dollars does seem a lot to spend on a dog," Harold said.

Christopher hurried back into the dining car carrying four plates of dessert. He stopped short when he heard Harold.

"Oh, Mrs. Rothchild," Christopher fretted as he set four plates of dessert on our table. "How many times have I asked you not to speak about Muffy's collar. It makes it hard for me to protect you when everyone around you…" Christopher trailed off, not finishing his thought.

Mrs. Rothchild laughed. "Oh, Christopher. You worry too much. This is my fourth time on this train, and nothing has ever happened to me before."

"Not to worry," Aunt Shirley said. "I'm a private investigator, and Garrett here is a cop."

All eyes turned to our table, and I could feel the heat from their gazes.

"You're a cop?" Floyd spat out the question to Garrett.

Garrett met his gaze straight on. "I am."

Floyd muttered something unintelligible under his breath, but I got the meaning.

"Please do not worry," Christopher said to Garrett. "We have our own security person on the train, and we've never had an incident of theft before."

Garrett nodded at Christopher. "Good to hear."

Garrett picked up his fork and took a small bite of the Tiramisu sitting in front of him.

He could pretend all he wanted, but I knew from the stiffness in Garrett's shoulders that he was aware of the trouble Mrs. Rothchild had just incurred on herself. She may not think others had nefarious plans, but I'd been around the block enough to know that that wasn't always true. And both Harold Walsh and Clive Salter had already intimated at having money problems.

Christopher finished passing out the desserts to everyone else, and I took turns eating both the double-chocolate cake and the tiramisu. By the time I polished off the desserts and another glass of champagne, I was stuffed and slightly tipsy.

"It's too early to turn in," Aunt Shirley said. "Let's go to the lounge and play some poker."

"I wouldn't mind joining you," Harold said. "I mean, if that's okay."

Aunt Shirley shrugged. "I don't see why not. Anyone else want to play?"

Clive grinned. "Don't mind if I do."

I looked over at Floyd. *Please say no. Please say no.*

"No," Floyd said gruffly.

"I wouldn't mind playing a couple hands," June said shyly. "It might be fun."

Floyd narrowed his eyes at June. "I said no."

June's face turned red, but she didn't say anything more.

"Well, I for one do not play *poker*." Angelica narrowed her eyes at her husband. "You have an early day tomorrow. Do not stay up late."

This time it was Harold Walsh's turn to look embarrassed. "I know what I have going on tomorrow."

Angelica smiled tightly. "Let's hope you do."

Without a backward glance, Angelica strode out of the dining car.

"Let's go," Floyd snarled at his wife. "I still don't trust that Delbert fella to stay out of our rooms. He just looks like a shifty character."

I rolled my eyes at Floyd's ridiculous statement as the two left the room.

"I thought he was a nice enough chap," Harold Walsh said with a mischievous smile. "He helped Angelica unpack all her toiletries without complaining once."

There was a light round of chuckles at that statement.

"Well, I'd love to play a couple hands of poker," Mrs. Rothchild said. "Are we playing for money?"

Clive cleared his throat and looked sideways at Garrett. "Well, Mrs. Rothchild, technically that would be public gambling, and I'm pretty sure it's against the law."

Mrs. Rothchild waved off Clive's explanation. "Nonsense. We'd only be playing for a few bills."

Garrett smiled and shook his head. "I'm afraid Clive is right. Technically we can't play for money."

Mrs. Rothchild frowned. "Then what do we play for?"

"Fun," Old Man Jenkins piped up then looked at Aunt Shirley. "And bragging rights."

"You wish, old man," Aunt Shirley said.

Harold looked at his watch. "You know, now that I think about it, it is getting late. I should probably head back to my sleeping car to prepare for my meeting tomorrow morning. Thank you all for a lovely evening. I will see you tomorrow."

I watched Harold walk out of the dining car. "And then there were six."

"What was that all about?" Mrs. Rothchild asked.

"I'd say since we aren't playing for money," Aunt Shirley said, "Harold isn't interested."

Clive clapped his hands together. "Looks like it's just the six of us. I say we hit the lounge and play a few hands."

Our lounge car was empty, except for Jack behind the bar. "Good to see you guys back again. What can I get you?"

"How about an Old Fashioned," Aunt Shirley said.

Mrs. Rothchild's face lit up. "Oh me, too! I haven't had one of those in *years.*"

Clive chuckled. "I like women who know how to drink."

"And the rest of you?" Jack asked.

I ordered a gin and tonic and looked around the room as the men placed their orders.

"There doesn't really seem to be a table conducive to playing a few hands," I observed.

"What kind of table do you need?" Jack asked as he slid me my drink.

"We were wanting to play a couple hands of poker," Mrs. Rothchild said.

Jack shrugged. "Well, I'm just pouring drinks. So if it's okay with you guys, I can also deal. You can sit up here at the bar and I can be your dealer."

Aunt Shirley winked at Jack. "You can deal poker *and* you're a bartender? Good thing I'm already married or I might just have to steal you away from here."

Jack laughed good-naturedly. Which was kind of him, seeing as how Aunt Shirley was probably a good forty-five years older. "Well, my girlfriend might have something to say about that." Jack reached under the counter and pulled out a deck of cards and a box of toothpicks and handed them to Aunt Shirley. "Go ahead and shuffle them up while I finish pouring drinks. I'm assuming you guys are playing for toothpicks?"

Aunt Shirley rolled her eyes at Garrett. "Looks that way."

"Excuse me," Delbert said suddenly appearing in the lounge doorway. I frowned at his appearance. He was beginning to sweat, and his face was deathly white. He looked dead on his feet. "I was about to turn in for the evening. I was wondering if anyone needed anything else? Would anyone like me to turn down their bed?"

I could swear his words were slurring.

"Been turning down my own bed since I was a kid," Clive joked. "I think I can take it from here."

Aunt Shirley laughed. "Me, too. I think the old man and I are good. Thanks for asking, Delbert."

"Delbert," Mrs. Rothchild said softly, "have you taken your blood pressure medicine?"

Delbert shook his head. "I'm getting ready to when I get to my cabin."

Mrs. Rothchild frowned. "You don't look too good."

Delbert smiled. "I'll be fine, Mrs. Rothchild." Delbert bit his lip and steady himself on his feet. "Are you sure there isn't anything else I can get you, Mrs. Rothchild? Do you need me to take Muffy's collar? It may not be safe for it to be out like this now that people know how much it's worth."

I narrowed my eyes at Delbert. Had he been standing around listening to our conversations and I hadn't noticed? He wasn't exactly being subtle about getting his hands on the expensive diamonds.

Mrs. Rothchild rubbed Muffy's face with her own. "Thank you, Delbert. But I think Muffy and I will be okay tonight."

Delbert frowned. "Very well, ma'am. As you know, Denver is my last stop. I guess I'll see you on your next trip with us, Mrs. Rothchild. It's always a pleasure when you travel with us."

Mrs. Rothchild smiled. "Thank you, Delbert. You give my best to your momma now, you hear?"

Delbert nodded gravely. "Yes, ma'am."

Delbert looked at Jack before slightly staggering out of the lounge doorway.

"You know his mom?" I asked.

Mrs. Rothchild laughed. "No, not really. But I've traveled the rails long enough to know a lot about the workers. At least, the ones in this section since it's the section I stay in. Delbert lives with his mom and takes care of her. Jack here has a girlfriend he loves but is having a hard time committing to—"

"I'm going to commit one of these days," Jack objected good naturedly.

Mrs. Rothchild snorted. "So you say. Christopher has a little sister that has some medical problems, and that's why he works so many hours on the train. He sends all his extra money to his family so he can help pay for his sister's treatments." Mrs. Rothchild leaned in closer. "And Mr. Barger has recently gone through a nasty divorce, but that's not why he's so mean and angry. He's been like that since he started working on the train."

I laughed at that. "I don't know who this Mr. Barger is, but you seem to know a lot about all the workers on this train."

"That she does," Jack said. "Mrs. Rothchild is a wonderful woman who cares about all of us."

Twenty minutes later, Mrs. Rothchild and I were almost out of toothpicks. Most of them were split pretty evenly between Aunt Shirley, Clive, and Garrett. Old Man Jenkins was barely hanging on.

"Can you bring Muffy a small dish of water?" Mrs. Rothchild asked Jack as she placed Muffy on the top of the bar.

Jack reached out and gave the dog a scratch under her chin. "You bet."

"Your dog is really well behaved around everyone," I said. "I never hear her bark or get loud."

Mrs. Rothchild's face brightened. "Oh, yes. Muffy is wonderful around people. Except for Mr. Barger. She doesn't really like him."

There's that Barger guy again.

Jack smiled as he set the bowl of water down in front of Muffy. "Not many people do."

"That's the second time you've mention a Mr. Barger," I said. "Who's this Barger guy?"

"Did someone just say my name?" a deep voice asked.

A man of average height and build stood in the doorframe. He had hard green eyes, and his dark blonde hair had a slight natural curl. He looked serious but relaxed in his dark blue suit. He brought his hands up to his waist…which gave us all a peek at his exposed gun.

"We were just talking about the great security on the train," Jack said smoothly.

"That's me. I keep the peace on this train and make sure no one does anything illegal." He walked over to where we were bellied up to the bar, toothpicks lined in front of us, cards being shuffled by Jack.

"What's going on over here?" Barger asked. "Nothing illegal, I hope."

"Just a friendly game of toothpick poker," Garrett answered casually.

Barger ran his eyes over us and then looked back at our pile of toothpicks. "It's against the law to play for money."

40

"Thank you, Captain Obvious," Aunt Shirley said. "You see any money being exchanged? We're using toothpicks."

Barger narrowed his eyes at Aunt Shirley, which caused Muffy to growl. Barger turned to face Mrs. Rothchild and Muffy. "Don't know why they allow dogs on this train."

"Because it's a free country," Mrs. Rothchild said as she tried to sooth Muffy.

Barger looked at Jack. "You know the rules."

Jack sighed. "They're playing for toothpicks. They aren't hurting anyone."

"I also heard there are some on this train who know what the dog's collar is worth," Barger said.

Garrett shrugged. "It was mentioned at dinner."

Barger shifted on his feet. "So there might be people interested in relieving Mrs. Rothchild of some of her valuables now that they know what she's worth."

Now why would he think that?

Jack furrowed his brow. "I don't know anything about that. But I can tell you that no one is taking advantage of Mrs. Rothchild. We're just having a little fun."

Barger scowled at Mrs. Rothchild. "I've never had trouble on my train before, and I don't intend to start now."

Aunt Shirley downed the last of her Old Fashioned. "Don't worry, Barger. If something happened, and you actually had to do something other than walk around and look like a wanna-be cop, there are people here who can help you out."

Barger's face turned red and a vein popped out on his forehead. "Excuse me?"

Aunt Shirley shrugged. "You got a *real* policeman and a *real* investigator on this train." She turned and looked at Garrett. "We're qualified and certified! Am I right?"

"I think she means certifiable," Garrett mumbled under his breath to me.

I giggled but didn't say anything. Aunt Shirley didn't need any help in the putting-someone-in-their-place category. It was just fun to sit back and watch the fireworks happen.

Barger's mouth twitched as he raked his gaze over Aunt Shirley. "*You're* police?"

Aunt Shirley crossed her arms over her sagging chest. "I ain't...but he is." She pointed to Garrett. "*I'm* the investigator. Been one for more years than you've been alive I'd venture."

Even though Barger was trying hard to steel his features, I could tell this bit of news took him by surprise. "Why wasn't I informed there would be law enforcement on this trip?"

"Because it's none of your business what my job is," Garrett said. "And I'm on my honeymoon."

Barger looked Garrett over. "Then I guess we can almost guarantee there won't be any surprises this train ride."

Aunt Shirley grinned. "One never knows."

CHAPTER 6

I opened my eyes and listened to the murmuring voices at the door. I had no idea what time it was, but since it was still dark in the room, I figured it must be early.

"Right now we have no idea what happened. I do know he takes medication for high blood pressure, so maybe a heart attack or stroke." There was a brief pause. "Or it could be intentional. I do know he hasn't been happy for a while now."

I recognized Christopher's voice.

"We're just asking everyone to stay in their cabins when we reach Denver until the police have a chance to take the body," Christopher continued.

"I understand," Garrett said. "Let me know if there's anything I can do to help out."

"Thank you, Mr. Kimble," Christopher said. "I'm sorry I had to wake you. Please go back to sleep."

The door softly clicked closed and I whirled around in the bed. "What's going on? Who's dead?"

Garrett shuffled back into bed. "Delbert. Looks like he may have had a heart attack or stroke."

I gasped. "Don't give me that. I heart Christopher say it also might be intentional. That makes no sense. He didn't act like he was going to kill himself last night when we talked with him. He said he'd see Mrs. Rothchild next time she was on the train."

Garrett gathered me close. "First off, he said Delbert took blood pressure medication. It could be he had a heart attack or stroke. And second, there's no telling about some people and why they might want to end their life."

I leaned up on one elbow. "You honestly don't believe that for one minute, do you? You can't honestly tell me that no warning bells aren't going off?"

Garrett grinned. "Warning bells? Is that private investigator talk?"

I rolled my eyes. "You know what I mean. Something's off here."

Garrett sighed. "I have no reason to believe anything is off. But, I'm sure you and Aunt Shirley will get to the bottom of it later. How about right now we just go back to sleep for a few hours? Christopher stopped by to tell us that we are not to leave the cabin until the Denver police take possession of the body. So that's that."

I plopped back down on my back. I wasn't happy with having to stay locked up inside the cabin. Okay, maybe not exactly locked up, but it felt like that when I wanted nothing more than to start questioning people who knew Delbert.

"I can see the wheels turning in your head," Garrett said. "I'm going to let you ponder while I go back to sleep."

"Good idea. No way am I going to be able to sleep now."

I waited a few minutes until I heard Garrett's deep, even breathing before I flung back the covers and tiptoed over to the chair by the window. I spread open the curtain and marveled at the beautiful sunrise. Digging through my bag, I brought out a pen and notebook. Settling in, I jotted down what I knew of Delbert. How he'd behaved yesterday, his demeanor at dinner and afterward, all the things Mrs. Rothchild had said about him helping his mom, and even the weird way he acted around the other workers. I also jotted down the fact he and Floyd Hughes had exchanged words.

Could someone have killed Delbert and made it look like a suicide? And if so...why?

I jotted down a few more questions then read over my list. Maybe I was jumping the gun a little, but something didn't seem quite right about Delbert's death. Of course, it could just be I was itching to find a story when there wasn't one. I looped the pen through the spiral notebook then set it aside. Tiptoeing back to the bed, I quietly slid in beside Garrett.

"Did you figure it out?" Garrett asked.

I let out a little scream of surprise and hit him on the shoulder. "You scared me. I thought you were asleep."

"I never sleep soundly. You know that."

I did know that. Too much of Garrett's past hindered his sleeping.

I snuggled against him. "Let's close our eyes for a little bit longer."

By the time Garrett and I awoke, breakfast was past being served and we were quickly approaching lunchtime. We stopped by Aunt Shirley and Old Man Jenkins's sleeping car, but no one was in. Opting for brunch in the lounge, we made our way up the stairs and into the viewing car.

I frowned when I saw Christopher and Barger huddled over someone or something. I couldn't tell from my angle what it was.

"Everything okay here?" Garrett asked.

The two men jerked up, then Christopher smiled when he saw us.

"Oh, Mr. and Mrs. Kimble," Christopher said. He put his finger to his lips then looked down at Mrs. Rothchild. "I was going to wake her and suggest she go back to her room, but she doesn't seem to want to wake up."

My heart fell to my stomach. I'd been around enough dead bodies this past year to know what that might mean. Surely there couldn't be two deaths on the train within a few hours of each other…could there? I was about to sprint over to Mrs. Rothchild when she suddenly opened her eyes and smiled at me.

"Oh good," Mrs. Rothchild said, totally unaware she'd just given me a heart attack. "I was hoping to stay awake long enough to talk with you and your new husband."

"You're okay?" I asked hesitantly. I still couldn't believe my eyes. And what exactly did that say about me and my life when my first assumption at seeing someone with their eyes closed is that they're dead?

Mrs. Rothchild laughed. "Of course I'm okay. Sad because of what happened to Delbert this morning, but physically I've never felt better."

"Then I'll be on my way," Barger said.

He strode through the viewing car past us and into coach.

"Perhaps you would be better off taking a nap in your car?" Christopher kindly suggested.

"Nonsense," Mrs. Rothchild said. "Muffy and I were just closing our eyes for a moment."

"Then can I offer you more tea?" Christopher asked.

"That would be lovely!" Mrs. Rothchild patted the seat next to her and motioned me over. "Usually Muffy and I go back to our

46

room after breakfast, but I so hoped I'd see you two young people again. It's been a long time since I hung out with newlyweds."

Garrett smiled at Christopher. "We've got it from here. We'll stay with her and keep watch."

Christopher gave Garrett a slight bow and patted Mrs. Rothchild on the shoulder. "I'll be right back with your tea." Christopher looked at me. "Did you or your husband want hot tea?"

I didn't have to look at Garrett to see his response to a suggestion of hot tea. "No thanks. We'll get something in the lounge in a few minutes."

"Very well," Christopher said before leaving.

Garrett and I went to sit next to Mrs. Rothchild and Muffy.

"I just can't believe Delbert is gone," Mrs. Rothchild said. "It's so unexpected."

"It does seem that way," I agreed. I didn't want to put words in Mrs. Rothchild's mouth, but I did want to know what she thought about the suicide angle or if she believed it was natural causes.

"He was such a nice man," Mrs. Rothchild went on. "He seemed to enjoy taking care of his mom." Mrs. Rothchild wiped a tear from her eye. "I wonder what the poor woman will do now?"

I patted Mrs. Rothchild on the arm. "I don't know. I heard Christopher say they weren't sure if he died from a heart attack or stoke...or if maybe he took his own life. It's odd he'd up and kill himself when he's needed as much as he is, don't you think?"

Garrett cleared his throat, but I ignored him.

"It does seem odd," Mrs. Rothchild said slowly. "But then, maybe he was dealing with things we didn't know about. I really only knew him on a superficial level."

So much for the murder theory.

"Maybe so," I agreed. "I'm probably reading more into it than I should. It might very well just be a heart attack or stroke."

"It's a beautiful view," Garrett suddenly said as he took in the panoramic view of the steep canyon and fast-moving river. "I can see why you take this trip often."

Mrs. Rothchild smiled sweetly. "My husband and I never had children of our own. And it gets very lonely in my house now that he's gone. I have a housekeeper that stays with me, but it's just not the same. So I like taking this trip because my husband was a rancher here in Colorado. When he died, I moved to Missouri to be closer to my sister."

"Can I ask you a question?" I asked Mrs. Rothchild.

"Anything."

I opened my mouth, but before I could say anything Christopher walked back into the viewing car with a to-go-cup of hot tea in his hands.

"Here you are, Mrs. Rothchild. Be careful, it's hot." Christopher gently handed Mrs. Rothchild the Styrofoam cup before straightening. "If you need help getting to your sleeping car, just let me know."

Mrs. Rothchild patted Christopher on the arm. "You're too kind. I should be okay for a little while."

Christopher absentmindedly scratched Muffy's head as he gave Garrett a pointed look.

"We'll make sure someone sees to her," Garrett assured Christopher.

Mrs. Rothchild watched Christopher head down the aisle and into the coach area of the train. "Such a nice young man. Always watching over me when I take this trip."

"I think he's just worried about you sleeping out here in the open," Garrett said. "Especially since Muffy is still wearing her high-dollar collar."

Mrs. Rothchild waved her hand in the air. "It's okay. Muffy will bark if someone comes too close and I'm sleeping."

I had my doubts about that. Muffy wasn't exactly a ferocious watchdog, no matter what Mrs. Rothchild wanted to believe.

"She didn't bark when Christopher and Barger tried to wake you and we were standing by watching," I said as gently as I could.

Mrs. Rothchild frowned. "You may be right. Of course, Muffy would never bark at Christopher. I guess that's the reason Muffy didn't bark when Mr. Barger and Christopher were around me. Muffy knows Christopher would never hurt me. But I suppose I should be more careful. It's just such a lovely view, and I was hoping to talk with you two. Take my mind off of what happened this morning."

Clive Salter lumbered up the stairs from the sleeping cars down below. "What's this I hear about a lovely view?"

Mrs. Rothchild laughed. "Clive, so nice to see you again."

Clive gave Mrs. Rothchild a wolfish grin then straddled a bench seat a few feet from where we were all sitting. "Thought I'd come up and see what everyone else was up to. Watch the lovely view."

He gave Mrs. Rothchild a wink, which caused her to blush and giggle.

Oh boy!

Clive Salter had to be a good ten years younger than Mrs. Rothchild. The fact he was in need of money didn't slip by me, either. While a part of me liked Clive and his larger-than-life laugh and jovial nature, there was no way I was gonna sit back and let him con Mrs. Rothchild out of her money.

"Garrett and I were about to head to the lounge to get a bite to eat," I said to Clive. "Care to join us?"

"Or you could stay here with me and keep me company for a few more minutes," Mrs. Rothchild said.

Clive gave her a slow smile. "I think I'd like that."

I gritted my teeth and was about to give Clive what-for when Garrett grabbed my hand. "Have fun. We'll see you soon, I'm sure."

Garrett helped me up from my chair and we made our way into the lounge. Harold and Angelica were seated in a booth, while Floyd was bellied up to the bar.

"Why did you let him stay with her?" I huffed. "Surely you know a con artist when you see one?"

Garrett chuckled. "Ryli, I don't even know where to start. Yes, I know a con artist when I see one. Yes, I'm sure Clive is being overly friendly for a reason, but I also know it's a train. It's not like he has anywhere to run if he does rob her blind—which I don't think he will. I actually like the guy."

I pursed my lips, not ready to let it go. Aunt Shirley and I had recently helped a group of elderly women out of a situation where they were being conned by a man preying on their hearts and their jewelry, and I didn't want to see the same thing happen to Mrs. Rothchild.

"Hello there," Jack called as Garrett and I entered the lounge. "Go ahead and sit wherever you like. What can I get you?"

"Coke?" Garrett asked me.

"Sure."

"Two Cokes please," Garrett said as he led me to a table by the window.

"Coming up," Jack called.

I nodded to Harold and Angelica as we passed their table. They didn't even acknowledge me, they were so deep in their conversation. Floyd was nursing a pretty stiff drink…June was nowhere around. I hoped she was okay and that Floyd hadn't berated her even more when they got back to the sleeping car last night.

I slid into a booth directly behind Harold, while Garrett slid across from me. He gave me a wink as he turned to survey the room. Always a cop.

"I wonder where Aunt Shirley and Old Man Jenkins are?" I said. "They weren't in their sleeping car, they weren't in the viewing car, and they aren't in here. Where else could they be?"

Garrett gave me a piercing look. "I'm sure they're around."

"Oh no!" I gasped. "What if they got off in Denver to stretch their legs and missed getting back on the train?"

CHAPTER 7

Garrett shook his head. "I doubt that happened. She would have called you on your cell if it did."

I scowled at him. "Then where are they?"

Jack set the drinks down in front of us. "Are you asking about your aunt and uncle?"

"Yes," I said. "Have you seen them?"

Jack chuckled. "They both came in after breakfast and had a couple drinks, then your aunt announced that since you both were going to stay inside and honeymoon the day away, she was going to go make new friends."

I groaned and covered my face with my hands.

Garrett laughed. "That sounds like Aunt Shirley."

Jack set down two straws. "She dragged a complaining husband out of the lounge and said the people in coach were probably fifty times friendlier than the stiffs in this room."

"That *definitely* sounds like Aunt Shirley," Garrett snorted.

I tried to give Garrett my evil eye, but he was totally right.

"Jack, what do you think of Delbert's sudden death?" I asked. "Do you think it was a heart attack or stroke?" I paused before adding, "Or maybe suicide?"

Jack shrugged. "Could be heart attack or stroke. I know he took medication. As far as the possibility of suicide, I wasn't that close to Delbert. I don't think anyone really was. He was kind of a loner. Kept to himself." Jack lightly slapped the table with one hand. "Let me know if you need anything else."

Garrett and I sat in silence and smiled at each other. I knew my face probably had a dopey look to it, but I didn't care. I couldn't believe that the man sitting across from me was mine until I died.

"What do you want me to do?" Harold hissed softly behind me.

"I don't care what you do, Mr. Big-Shot Investment Guy," Angelica hissed back, "but you better do something. Not only did you lose our friends' money, but you lost *our* money. I'm *not* going to live the rest of my life in poverty. You made this mess, you better clean it up. If you don't, I'm done. I'll leave you the minute this train pulls into Kansas City if you don't think of some way to get everyone's money back."

Harold sucked in his breath. I looked at Garrett to see if he was hearing the conversation, but he had pulled out his cell phone and was scrolling through.

"You don't mean that," Harold whined.

"I've never meant anything more in my life," Angelica said coldly. "I'm going back to the sleeper car. Don't bother returning until you have a plan."

I heard a small commotion behind me and figured Angelica was gathering up her purse and leaving. I gently kicked Garrett under the table. He looked up questioningly from his phone. I gave him the big eyes, but unlike Aunt Shirley, he had no idea what I was trying to say.

"Did you hear that?" I mouthed, not wanting Harold to know I heard every word.

"What?" Garrett asked in a regular voice.

I gave him the big eyes again—any bigger and they would pop out of my head! I obviously needed to school Garrett on how non-verbal conversation worked.

"Have you given anymore thought about this PI business with Aunt Shirley?" Garrett asked.

I sighed. "No. I mean, it would be exciting, but I'm scared. What if I'm bad at being a private investigator?"

Garrett smiled. "Don't tell Aunt Shirley I said this, but I think she's doing a fine job training you."

"Hey, there you two love birds are," Aunt Shirley called from the lounge doorway. She grabbed hold of her huge oversized purse and shuffled over to our table. "I was afraid you'd gone and died in that sleeping car."

"Not that lucky," Garrett mumbled…then gave me an innocent grin when he saw me scowl.

I scooted over so Aunt Shirley could sit by me, and Garrett did the same for Old Man Jenkins. Aunt Shirley was looking dapper today in her Day-Glo pink 'Go Ahead, Punk, Make My Day' t-shirt with matching pink and purple hair stripes. I was used to this Aunt Shirley. A few weeks before she'd colored her hair to match my wedding colors: burgundy, orange, and purple. That had been a little much.

"So, I decided my awesomeness needed to be spread around and went to shine my light over in coach," Aunt Shirley said as she waved her hand to get Jack's attention.

"What can I get ya?" Jack called out.

"Margarita on the rocks for me," Aunt Shirley said.

"I'll just have a water," Old Man Jenkins said.

Aunt Shirley rolled her eyes. "It's like I married a teetotaler!"

I giggled and took a sip of my Coke.

"I just don't feel the need to drink twenty-four seven," Old Man Jenkins corrected.

"Why not, there doesn't seem to be anything more to do," Aunt Shirley said. "I've decided maybe train life isn't the life for me."

Garrett snorted. "I figured it would take about a day before you realized you'd be miserable."

"I hate to admit it, Ace, but you're right," Aunt Shirley said. "There's not a lot to do here. I'm bored stiff. I need to spread my wings and fly. Chase down a bad guy, wrestle him to the ground, and then maybe shoot him if I feel like it."

Harold choked on his drink. Aunt Shirley and I half turned in our seats to look at him.

"Sorry," Harold said. "I feel like I'm always eavesdropping. Sounds like you lead an interesting life."

"You know it," Aunt Shirley bragged. "And right about now I'm missing it. There's not a lot of action on this train."

"Sometimes action can be overrated," Harold said cryptically. "But there has been a little commotion. That Delbert fella dying this morning."

Aunt Shirley shrugged. "Yeah, I guess so. But a medical death or even a suicide isn't anything we can investigate. I mean, we pretty much know how he died. Either his heart gave out, or he took his own life."

Did he?

I was surprised how accepting Aunt Shirley was being about Delbert's death. Usually the woman looked twenty different ways at a situation. Why did she believe Delbert's death was so cut and dry? And why, for that matter, did I think maybe there was more to it than that? I was never the one that wanted to see more into a situation.

"Speaking of action," Aunt Shirley said. "How did your meeting go this morning?"

A look I couldn't identify passed over Harold's face, but I saw his jaw flex. "Not as well as I had hoped." His lips barely moved when he spoke the words.

"Sorry to hear that," Old Man Jenkins said. "I know you were hoping for good results."

Harold nodded then picked up his drink and took a long swallow.

Thwack!

I looked over at the bar in surprise, and Jack gave me a self-conscious smile and held up a dangerous looking tool. "Sorry. We're trying to keep with the authenticity of the time, so when ice is needed I have to chop it with this ice pick."

"Holy cow," I said. "That looks dangerous."

Jack gave the block of ice one more chop, slivers of ice flying everywhere.

"Only in your hands, dear," Garrett joked.

I stuck my tongue out at him and he laughed.

Jack came over and brought Aunt Shirley her margarita and Old Man Jenkins his water. "What about you two, can I get you a sandwich or something?"

I looked at the small menu board next to the wall. "I think I'll have the Reuben with Jalapeno chips."

Aunt Shirley cackled. "Not worried about your breath now that you've snagged a husband I see!"

I felt my face heat up. "Could you, for *once*, pretend you have a filter and use it?"

Aunt Shirley scrunched up her face as though thinking. "Nope."

Garrett chuckled and shook his head. "I'll have the same thing."

He winked at me, and I was almost tempted to suggest we ditch the food and go back to the sleeping car.

"By the way," Old Man Jenkins said. "As we were making our way to the lounge, we saw Mrs. Rothchild and her dog sleeping in the viewing car."

Garrett frowned. "Did you see Clive? He's supposed to be keeping her company."

"Nope," Aunt Shirley said. "Only person we saw was Mrs. Rothchild."

Harold cleared his throat. "It was nice talking to you all. I better head back to my room and see how Angelica is doing."

He jumped up from his booth and nodded to us before walking briskly out of the lounge.

"You got any pretzels I don't have to pay for?" Floyd called drunkenly from the end of the bar.

"No," Jack said. "But can I get you something to eat to go with the drink?" Jack asked.

Floyd snorted. "You people are charging an arm and a leg for a simple sandwich. It's highway robbery is what that is. Don't think I don't know that's why you don't open the dining car. You gotta rake us over the coals somehow."

I rolled my eyes at Aunt Shirley. The man gets a free ride on a train and he has nothing better to do than gripe about the sandwich he may have to buy.

Jack grabbed two bags of chips off the rack and tossed them on the plates before walking over to where we were sitting. "Here you go, two Reuben sandwiches and chips."

"Thanks, Jack," I said. I quickly lifted my sandwich and took a very unlady-like bite. I hadn't realized until he'd set the sandwiches down how ravenous I really was.

Floyd suddenly stood and staggered over to where we were. He grabbed hold of our table to keep from face planting onto the floor.

"You might want to lay off the booze," Garrett said quietly as Floyd passed our table.

I knew that voice, and I knew Floyd should be scared.

"Phht," Floyd said. "Maybe you need to mind your own business. We ain't in your town, copper. You ain't got no right to tell me what I can and can't do."

Garrett put his sandwich down and Old Man Jenkins got out of the booth. Without a word, Garrett also slid out of the booth and stood a few feet in front of Floyd. Beads of sweat popped out on Floyd's forehead, but he lifted his chin in anger.

Garrett crossed his arms over his expansive chest and chuckled. "Thing is, Floyd, I actually *can* tell you what to do. But just to keep it fun, it wouldn't be me doing the dirty work." Garrett looked over his shoulder and grinned at Aunt Shirley. "Did you not just hear this mean old women say she was itching to take someone down?"

58

Aunt Shirley jumped out of the booth and positioned herself in a fighting stance. "Whoowhee! Let me at him!"

CHAPTER 8

"This train is full of a bunch of freaks," Floyd said as he stumbled to the doorway of the train.

"Did you see how scared he was?" Aunt Shirley cackled as she turned to give me a high-five. "He tucked tail and ran!"

Garrett chuckled and sat down in the booth, Old Man Jenkins following suit.

"He sure did," Garrett said. "Let's just hope he doesn't take it out on June."

I sobered instantly. "Do you think he will?"

Garrett shrugged. "Hard to say."

Tears filled my eyes. "I hate that for her. She seems like a nice lady. How in the heck did she get stuck with someone like Floyd?"

Aunt Shirley finished off the last of her margarita. "Maybe she lost a bet. That's the story I'm telling people now when they ask me why I married the old man here."

I chuckled, picked up a chip, and slowly chewed. My heart hurt for June and the awful marriage she was obviously in. I gave Garrett a wink. "Thank you for being a good one."

Garrett winked back. "Thank you for not being crazy." He looked pointedly at Aunt Shirley when he said it.

Old Man Jenkins laughed.

"Aunt Shirley, don't you think it's odd that Delbert up and died last night?" I asked.

Aunt Shirley shrugged. "If he died from his heart giving out, or he died because he took his own life...either way, it doesn't seem like foul play."

I shook my head. "But last night he told us all he'd see Mrs. Rothchild on her next trip."

Aunt Shirley put her hand over mine. "Honey, sometimes things happen we don't understand. And believe me, if I thought something was off about the death, I'd say something."

"But you don't?" I asked meekly.

"Who gained from his death?" Aunt Shirley asked.

I furrowed my brow. "What?"

"That's a good question," Garrett said.

I thought about it. As far as I knew, no one on the train benefitted from Delbert's death. He didn't seem to have money to leave to anyone. He didn't really even seem to have friends to leave anything to.

"I guess you're right," I said. "I'm just not used to this kind of a death. Usually our deaths aren't so cut and dry."

Garrett smiled. "That's an odd statement. But I get what you're saying."

I blew out a breath. "Okay. So I guess maybe I'm trying to find something that isn't there. I just wanted to see what Aunt Shirley thought."

"That's why we're gonna make a great team!" Aunt Shirley exclaimed.

I cut my eyes to Garrett but neither one of us said anything.

"Hey," Aunt Shirley said suddenly. "I have something for us."

"For us?" I asked. "Like you and me?"

"Yep." She pulled out a card from her huge purse and slapped it on the table. "I had these made up before we left. What do you think?"

I gingerly picked up the card from the table…almost scared of what I'd find. I looked down at the card in my hand. It was a business card.

'Andrews & Sinclair-Kimble Investigators

Have questions you need answers to…just ASK!'

"Wow," I said shakily, handing the card to Garrett. "You made business cards."

"Now don't go getting all panicky on me," Aunt Shirley snapped. "I told you we were moving forward with this. The only thing you have left to do to become a certified private investigator is take the test. Easy-peasy."

"I see you're keeping your maiden name," Old Man Jenkins said dryly.

"Of course," Aunt Shirley snapped. "It would sound ridiculous if I used your name. We couldn't do the whole 'ask' thing. It would be 'just ajsk' and that's just dumb."

I laughed and had to agree. Technically it wouldn't work.

It was suddenly very real for me. Aunt Shirley and I were going to go into business together as private investigators.

"God help the community," Garrett mumbled as he handed me back the business card. But I saw the twinkle in his eye. I knew he was on my side.

"Oh, hush," Aunt Shirley said. "We're gonna be awesome investigators. I've been teaching her all I know."

Old Man Jenkins and Garrett looked at each other but said nothing.

Smart men.

"I don't plan on giving up my job with Hank at the *Granville Gazette*," I said. "I still need to bring in an income."

Garrett opened his mouth, but I cut him off. "I still need to bring in an income. It's important to me. I want to contribute to our household."

"Like I've said before," Garrett said, "you could bag groceries for all I care. In fact, I prefer that. It would be less harmful to you and to my heart."

I reached over and laid my hand over his. "You've been teaching me how to shoot, Hank has taught me self-defense moves, and Aunt Shirley...well, Aunt Shirley has taught me a lot about how to escape from dangerous situations."

Garrett and Old Man Jenkins groaned.

"Well, she has," I said. "If you knew half the things we've gotten ourselves into, you'd never let me out of the house."

Garrett narrowed his eyes at Aunt Shirley. "Just when I think I'm settled and okay with her decision, I hear this and it makes me rethink everything."

"Oh, hush," Aunt Shirley said. "I've never gotten her in too much trouble."

Let's see, there was the kidnapping at Paige's wedding, the hostage situation in your old apartment from your neighbors, the countless breaking and enterings we've committed, and just recently you took a bullet to save Old Man Jenkins. We get in plenty of trouble!

"Yeah," I assured Garrett with a straight face. "Rarely are we in over our heads that much."

"I was there for your bachelorette party in Vegas, remember?" Garrett said. "The whole hiding-in-the-bathroom scene is still fresh in my mind."

I snickered and stuffed a chip in my mouth. "Let's finish the sandwiches and check on Mrs. Rothchild."

We sat in silence as Garrett and I finished our sandwiches. With a promise to stop in for a cocktail before dinner, we left Jack alone to finish clearing our table.

Mrs. Rothchild was sitting where we'd left her, her body angled in an uncomfortable pose. I could hear her snores from where I was standing. Muffy's head was buried in Mrs. Rothchild's lap.

"She looks peaceful," I said. "Are you sure we should wake her?"

Garrett made his way over to Mrs. Rothchild. "Yes. She may look peaceful, but the way her body's angled, she's going to wake up sore."

"Where's Christopher?" I asked. "He's usually hovering over her."

"He's running back and forth between coach and taking care of us," Aunt Shirley said. "I saw him in coach when we were leaving and going to the lounge."

Garrett bent down and gently shook Mrs. Rothchild's shoulder. "Mrs. Rothchild, are you awake?"

Mrs. Rothchild slowly blinked her eyes open. "Goodness. Did I fall asleep again?"

"Looks that way," I said.

Mrs. Rothchild patted her hair and sat up straighter in her chair, causing Muffy to poke her head up and look around. "I don't

64

know what's wrong with me this morning. Looks like Muffy and I both went back to sleep."

The Maltese gave a little yip then shot up and gave Mrs. Rothchild a slobbery lick on her cheek. Mrs. Rothchild laughed and squeezed her dog in a tight hug.

"We were all about to go back to our rooms and view some of this amazing scenery outside and probably take a little nap." I reached over and gave Muffy a scratch on her head. "Why don't you let us help you downstairs to your sleeping cabin?"

"That's probably a good idea," Mrs. Rothchild said.

I moved my hand down Muffy's neck and gasped.

"What's wrong, Ryli?" Garrett asked.

"Muffy's collar is gone!"

CHAPTER 9

"Gone?" Mrs. Rothchild cried as she pulled Muffy close to her chest and felt around the dog's neck. "Oh, my goodness! You're right! Muffy's been robbed!"

Had the situation not been so dire, I'd have laughed at her statement.

Garrett let out a soft curse behind me.

"Whoohoo!" Aunt Shirley cried. "We got ourselves a mystery to solve! See, *this* isn't cut and dry."

I gave her my best let's-try-and-be-subtle eye stare, but Aunt Shirley ignored me.

"How could this have happened?" Mrs. Rothchild sniffed. "I've never had a problem before." She looked around frantically. "Where's Christopher?"

I walked to the far end of the viewing car and peered into the coach passenger car. "I think I see Christopher. He must still be helping out in coach."

"You better go get him," Old Man Jenkins said solemnly.

"We'll stay here with Mrs. Rothchild." Garrett sat down next to the older woman.

I pushed opened the connecting doors and rushed through the tiny breezeway and into coach. It was a pretty nice setup for coach seating. The western theme, of course, ran throughout the car, but the seats were definitely more modern. Two chairs made up each row, and each of the plush, burgundy seats reclined. The windows were large and gave the passengers the impression of one continuous piece of glass.

I caught Christopher's eye and he blinked in surprise.

"Can I help you, Mrs. Kimble?" Christopher asked.

"I'm afraid it's Mrs. Rothchild. We have a little problem."

Christopher gasped. "What kind of problem? I haven't checked on Mrs. Rothchild for about half an hour now. Is she okay?"

I held up my hand. "She's okay physically, it's just…" I trailed off and looked around. I didn't want the other passengers to overhear, so I motioned him toward the end of the car. I leaned and lowered my voice. "I'm afraid Mrs. Rothchild has been robbed. Someone took Muffy's collar."

"No!" Christopher's mouth fell open and he staggered backward. "What should we do?"

"As much as it pains me to say this, I think we need to get the security officer involved."

Christopher pulled himself up to full height. "You're right. I'll take care of this right away. I'll have him go to your viewing car. We're in luck that the dining car is closed for lunch, so no one will be trekking back and forth through your viewing car. I'll make sure the passengers in coach go to the other lounge if they need lunch."

I placed my hand on Christopher's arm. "Thank you. Mrs. Rothchild is very upset and has asked for you when you get a chance."

"I'm on it."

Christopher turned and headed toward the front of the train while I opened the doors and walked through the tiny breezeway back into the viewing car. I figured Aunt Shirley and I would only have a couple minutes to question Mrs. Rothchild before Barger muscled his way in.

"I think I remember seeing a lot of people walking in and out of the viewing car," Mrs. Rothchild was saying as I skidded to a halt in front of her seat.

Aunt Shirley had already begun questioning Mrs. Rothchild. I looked over at Garrett, but he seemed content to let Aunt Shirley take the lead. I had to wonder if he was sizing up our ability to investigate.

"Of course, the only ones that stopped and spoke to me outside of you and Garrett was Clive," Mrs. Rothchild continued as she wrung her hands together. "All the others passed by without so much as a wave. These young people today…so self-centered and always in a hurry."

I suppressed a smile as I looked at Garrett. "Christopher is getting the security officer, Barger."

I caught the non-spoken look that passed between Aunt Shirley and Garrett.

"What's going on in here?" Barger demanded as he strode through the coach car and into our viewing car, Christopher close at his heels. "I hear there's been a robbery."

"That's correct," Garrett said.

"And where were the four of you at the time of the robbery?" Barger demanded.

Garrett lifted one corner of his mouth. "Well, since no one has established a time as to when the theft occurred, I'd say it would be hard to give an alibi."

Snap!

Garrett 1...Barger 0.

Barger's face flushed. "Right. I'm getting to that." He turned to Mrs. Rothchild. "I knew this would happen one day. Didn't I warn you about telling everyone about Muffy's collar?"

"You know, Barger," Aunt Shirley said. "You're about as loveable and huggable as a thorny cactus."

I slid a grin to Old Man Jenkins. He, too, looked just as amused.

Mrs. Rothchild sniffed back her tears. "I quite agree. You don't need to speak to me like that."

"I don't think there's any reason for you four to stay here," Barger said. "Christopher and I can take care of this. You need to return to your sleeping cars, and I will be down to take statements shortly."

"He's right," Garrett when Aunt Shirley started to argue. "We should probably go to our rooms."

Aunt Shirley's brows furrowed, and I knew she wanted to argue with Garrett...but I saw the subtle shake of Garrett's head.

"I agree," I added.

"Fine," Aunt Shirley huffed. "We'll go back to our sleeping cars."

"Thank you all for staying with me," Mrs. Rothchild said as Muffy licked the tears off Mrs. Rothchild's face.

"Are you sure you're gonna be okay?" I asked Mrs. Rothchild. I knew Garrett wanted us to leave, but I couldn't help but worry about Mrs. Rothchild's state of mind.

Mrs. Rothchild looked up adoringly at Christopher. "I'll be fine now that Christopher is here."

"I'm so sorry for leaving you," Christopher said. "A passenger got sick in coach, and I said I'd cover while the attendant on duty took care of the passenger."

Mrs. Rothchild reached up and patted Christopher on the arm. "You mustn't get worked up over it. Who knew someone would choose now to steal my necklace."

Barger muttered something unintelligible under his breath.

I looked at Aunt Shirley and frowned.

"I don't want to have to ask you again to leave," Barger said as he placed his hands on his hips—weapon exposed.

"Point taken," Old Man Jenkins said as he guided a loudly protesting Aunt Shirley down the aisle toward the stairs that would lead to our sleeping cabins.

Garrett put his hand on my elbow and gently guided me behind Aunt Shirley and Old Man Jenkins. I bit my lip and tried not to protest having to leave the scene of the crime the way Aunt Shirley was doing. I didn't always like how close Aunt Shirley and I were in attitude and personality. I was afraid it was like looking in the mirror forty years in the future.

We all stopped in front of our sleeping car. "We need to walk through this and figure out who was where," Aunt Shirley said.

Garrett nodded. "Agreed. I say we meet in our cabin in about fifteen minutes. There's no way I'm leaving this to that incompetent fool Barger to solve this case. He no more knows how to solve a crime than—"

"Ryli here knows how to cook," Aunt Shirley joked.

"Hey!" I exclaimed.

Garrett chuckled. "I wasn't going to say that."

"Oh, but you don't deny it!" I exclaimed.

Garrett pulled me close and kissed the top of my head. "Like I said, you two come back to our room in about fifteen minutes. And remember, don't say anything to anyone. I don't want to give anyone a heads up on what has happened or that we're going to help push this along."

"Even if tortured I won't tell a soul," Aunt Shirley said solemnly.

I rolled my eyes at Old Man Jenkins. Aunt Shirley…always the drama queen!

CHAPTER 10

"You really don't think Barger can solve this?" I asked Garrett once we entered our sleeping car.

Garrett let out a bark. "No, I don't think he can solve this. I don't think the man could find his way out of a paper bag."

I frowned. "I think either you or Hank once said the same thing about me and my ability to solve crimes."

Garrett chuckled. "That sounds like something Hank would say...not me."

I narrowed my eyes at him. "You better hope it was Hank.

Garrett threw up his hands and gave me a wicked grin. "Babe. Does that sound like me?"

"Yes! It totally sounds like you."

Garrett winked at me and headed toward the tiny bathroom. "I'm gonna take a quick shower. Usually that helps me process and think."

"I'd offer to scrub your back, but I think I'm kinda mad at you right now," I pouted.

Garrett said nothing...just gave me a wolfish grin.

I got out my pen and paper for Aunt Shirley. She'd want me to take notes as she spouted her theories. I made sure four tiny bottles of water were in the mini fridge and then set out a bag of pretzels I brought with us.

I frowned when a knock sounded at the door. By my calculations, Aunt Shirley was about ten minutes early. I flung open the door.

"You're early," I said.

"Shh. C'mon. We only have a few minutes."

"Where are we going?" I asked as Aunt Shirley dragged me down the narrow passageway.

"I found out where Delbert's sleeping car is. I think you're right. We need to eliminate every possible angle."

I grinned as we tiptoed up the steps. Looked like my instincts were paying off.

"Christopher and Barger are still talking to Mrs. Rothchild," Aunt Shirley whispered. "We need to surreptitiously get into coach and go to where sleeping car C section is. Evidently he had a car in that area of the train."

"How did you find this out?" I asked.

"I may have done a little digging while in coach this morning."

I chuckled. "I *knew* you had to be suspicious."

Aunt Shirley shushed me again then grabbed hold of my hand and duck walked me to the door leading into coach.

"Hey!" Barger suddenly yelled. "I told you to stay in your cabin!"

"Hurry," Aunt Shirley hissed.

She pried the door open and we rushed into coach. I looked over my shoulder and caught Barger heading toward us.

"Go! Go!" I cried, pushing against Aunt Shirley's back.

We threw out apologies to the people around us as we jumped and weaved in between the passengers. We reached the door leading into the viewing car of area C and shoved open the doors. There were about eight people milling around in the viewing car area. When we reached the stairs the led down to

73

sleeping car Section C, I glanced over my shoulder but didn't see Barger.

"Let's go see how innocent Delbert's death was," Aunt Shirley said.

We crept down the stairs but didn't see anyone out in the corridor. "He should be the first door like Christopher."

I groaned. "*Should* be? Do you know which sleeping car is his?"

Aunt Shirley grinned, causing her false teeth to pop out of her mouth. She quickly shoved them back in and squatted down in front of Delbert's supposed door. Opening her purse, she dug around and then yanked out a clear, flat package.

"Ta da!" Aunt Shirley cried. "Lock pick."

I looked around and made sure no one was coming. "Hurry, we don't have much time."

A few seconds later I heard a click.

"We're in," Aunt Shirley announced.

We silently entered Delbert's room. It was pretty much set up like mine, except the bed was smaller, and there was only one chair by the window.

"What are we looking for?" I asked.

Aunt Shirley shrugged. "I don't know. Something that looks out of place."

"I'll take the bathroom," I said.

I opened the bathroom door and took in my surroundings. I popped open the shower door. It was empty except for a small bar of soap. Nothing odd there…Delbert had been bald. I gave a cursory glance to the toilet and moved to the sink. Typical products like deodorant, toothbrush, and toothpaste. Again, nothing out of the ordinary.

"I might have something," Aunt Shirley called.

I ran out of the bathroom to where she was leaned over Delbert's night stand.

"What is it?" I asked.

"First off, did you find Delbert's blood pressure medicine?"

I frowned. "Actually, I don't remember seeing it."

Aunt Shirley smiled. "It's not here, either."

"Maybe the police took it?"

Aunt Shirley shrugged. "Could be. But do you know what I did find?"

"What?" I hissed, losing my patience.

"Take a look at this." She pointed to a clear spot.

"What?"

"You don't see it?" Aunt Shirley asked.

I leaned down and took a closer look. "You mean this white powder? What? You're thinking he was doing drugs?"

Aunt Shirley let out a barking laugh. "No. I think maybe someone crushed up some pills right here but didn't get them all brushed off."

"That's a pretty far leap," I said.

"Perhaps, but it may go to possible murder weapon. Quick, hand me my purse."

I grabbed hold of the monstrous object and hurled it at her. She dug around and pulled out a clear, plastic baggie.

"What's that?" I asked.

"Evidence bag," Aunt Shirley announced. "I've done some shopping now that I know we're going to be private investigators together."

I bit my lip, but didn't say a word. I watched silently as she scooped a tiny pile together and pushed it into the plastic bag, then shoved the evidence bag back inside her purse.

"Okay. Let's not say anything to the guys about this until we know for sure there was foul play involved with Delbert's death."

I frowned. "I thought we agreed we couldn't think of a motive to kill Delbert?"

"Not right now, but we may come up with something later. We need to head out. We've been here too long as it is."

We quickly exited the room and made our way upstairs. After a cursory glance, and no sign of Barger, we raced through the viewing car, through the coach section, and popped out into our viewing car area.

Still no sign of Barger.

"Should we be nervous we haven't seen Barger?" I asked.

Aunt Shirley shrugged. "Let's just get back to our cabin. See if the boys are together yet."

CHAPTER 11

I'd just closed the door behind me when Garrett walked out of the bathroom pulling on his t-shirt. He stopped short when he saw Aunt Shirley and me ogling him.

Garrett sighed. "Should I be worried the two of you just came from outside this cabin? You know, since we were given strict orders not to leave."

I looked at Aunt Shirley and we both shook our heads, trying to maintain our innocence.

Garrett sighed again. "That's what I figured."

There was a knock on the door, followed by Old Man Jenkins whispering for us to open up.

"Ryli, get your pen and paper ready," Aunt Shirley said.

I hid my smile behind the notebook and took a seat on the bed, leaving the two swivel chairs near the window vacant for Aunt Shirley and Old Man Jenkins. Garrett sat next to me on the bed.

"I set out some pretzels and the water's in the refrigerator." I flipped to an empty page in the notebook. "Help yourself."

Aunt Shirley waved her hand in the air. "I already have margaritas coming to us."

"How?" I asked. "You haven't been anywhere near the lounge."

Aunt Shirley's eyes sparkled. "I sent Jack a text before I came to pick you up and told him we needed refreshments...stat!"

Garrett shook his head in bewilderment. "When did you get Jack's cell number?"

Old Man Jenkins rolled his eyes. "This morning before she chatted up the coach section."

Aunt Shirley jumped up from her chair when a knock sounded at the door. "Is that you, Jack?"

"Yes, ma'am. Got your drinks right here."

Aunt Shirley opened the door and motioned Jack inside. "Did you see Barger? Did you get any grief from him?"

Jack grinned and set the pitcher of margarita on the small table under the window. "A little. But I can handle Barger. He was coming out of June and Floyd's room just now when I saw him." He straightened and looked pointedly at Garrett. "I hope you guys can solve this case for Mrs. Rothchild. That woman is a gem. She doesn't deserve this kind of pain."

"Understood," Garrett said. "We'll do our best."

"We sure will," Old Man Jenkins agreed.

I was glad to see Old Man Jenkins getting into the spirit of solving the case.

Jack left and Aunt Shirley poured rounds for all of us.

"I'm not really a margarita guy," Garrett said when Aunt Shirley handed him a glass.

"Just hush up and take it," Aunt Shirley demanded.

Garrett frowned, but he took the glass then turned to me. "So where do you want to start?"

"Me?" I said him. "This is Aunt Shirley's baby."

Garrett took a tentative drink of his margarita. "It's not bad."

Aunt Shirley preened. "Told ya so, Ace. You need to learn to trust me more."

78

Garrett snickered. "Doubtful." Garrett turned to me and lowered his hand to my arm. "No, Ryli. If you are going to start work as a private investigator, you need to learn proper procedure and protocol."

I took a deep breath, held it, then let it out slowly. When that didn't give me an epiphany, I took a slow swallow of my margarita, hoping to stall.

"Well?" Aunt Shirley demanded. "I'm not getting any younger."

"Fine. I'll start with the timeline and who had access to Mrs. Rothchild." I started writing down names. "We have Harold and Angelica in the lounge. We know the collar was still on Muffy when we first saw them. Angelica left first in a rage, followed later by Harold."

"But did you notice *when* Harold left?" Garrett asked me.

"No."

"He left the minute he heard Mrs. Rothchild was alone in the viewing car."

My mouth dropped open. "You remember that?"

Garrett smiled placatingly at me. "I'm a police chief. It's my job to remember these things."

"And we know that they are having financial problems," Aunt Shirley added. "Harold has all but admitted it."

I nodded my head. "And I heard them arguing this morning when they were in the lounge, and Angelica said if he didn't think of a plan to get money soon, she was going to divorce him."

"Interesting," Aunt Shirley said as I continued writing down information about Harold and Angelica.

"By the way," I said as I turned to Garrett. "You need to learn to read my body language better. I was trying to get you to listen in on the argument, and you were playing on your phone."

Garrett shook his head. "I heard every word. Unlike you, I didn't want to be obvious with my big eyes and head jerks."

I stuck my tongue out at him while Aunt Shirley and Old Man Jenkins snorted with laughter.

Garrett winked at me. I decided to ignore him and continued on with my timeline. "We know that Clive was with Mrs. Rothchild for an extended period of time. We left him alone with her, and we learned later he left her and went back to his room. We need to find out more about why he left. Plus we know he's having financial problems, also."

I put a star next to Clive's name to remind myself to ask him where he'd went and why he left Mrs. Rothchild alone.

"What about that horse's butt Floyd?" Aunt Shirley said. "We know he was in the lounge, but left later on. He could have taken it."

I wrote down Floyd's name. "I think that's it."

"What about June?" Garrett asked.

I furrowed my brow. "June? What about her?"

"We need to find out where she was," Garrett said. "*We* haven't personally seen her, but that doesn't mean she wasn't around during the time of the robbery."

"Garrett's right," Aunt Shirley said. "Where's June? Why haven't we seen her this morning? Did she eat early then go back to her cabin? Where exactly is she? We need to check out everyone."

I wrote down June's name. "I think that's it. We've talked about Harold, Angelica, Clive, Floyd, and June."

"Nope," Garrett said.

"Who else?" I asked.

"Christopher," Aunt Shirley said as she looked pointedly at Garrett. "It's awful convenient he left the viewing car at exactly the moment Mrs. Rothchild was robbed. He's hardly left her side this whole trip, and the minute he does, she's robbed."

"You think Christopher took the collar and then just happened to be called over to cover coach?" I asked.

Aunt Shirley shrugged. "Maybe. Which would be a lucky alibi for him. Otherwise he'd have had a difficult time explaining how the collar disappeared on his watch."

I nodded slowly. "And last night Mrs. Rothchild said Christopher sends money to his family so his sister can get the medical attention she needs. Maybe something has happened and he needs to get his hands on some quick money."

"Good thinking," Aunt Shirley said.

I added Christopher to the ever-growing list. "Now we have everyone."

"Not exactly," Aunt Shirley said.

I looked at my list and frowned. "Who else is there? We know Jack never left the lounge, so he didn't steal it."

"Unless he had an accomplice," Old Man Jenkins pointed out.

"That's true," Garrett agreed. "We may need to look into that later on."

"Then who?" I asked exasperatingly.

"Barger," Aunt Shirley said.

I blinked in surprise. "Barger? As in the security officer for the train?"

Garrett nodded. "Could be. He knows the ins and outs of the train, knows Mrs. Rothchild well enough to know her patterns."

"Plus we know he's recently gone through a nasty divorce," Aunt Shirley said. "I bet nasty also means expensive."

I frowned. "But wouldn't Muffy have barked if Barger got too close?"

Old Man Jenkins shook his head. "I don't think Muffy is quite the watch dog that Mrs. Rothchild believes. She's a very energetic and happy dog. All the people on this train and the dog never really reacts differently."

I thought about Muffy and her spastic loving ways. Old Man Jenkins was probably right. Mrs. Rothchild had probably never been in a situation like she was now. Who's to say how Muffy would have responded.

Garrett sighed. "I also hate to say it, but we need to look at Mrs. Rothchild herself."

My mouth dropped open. "What? Are you serious? Why on earth would she steal her own collar? And—and well, why?"

"Insurance," Aunt Shirley and Old Man Jenkins said at the same time.

Garrett nodded and took another sip of his margarita. "We have to include her because she did have access to the collar."

"She always has access to the collar," I argued.

"But for insurance purposes," Garrett said, "it would be easy to claim a theft took place if it was done in public. She made sure everyone knew about the collar, and then the very next day it's stolen. That, too, seems convenient."

"I don't like this one bit." I hastily added Mrs. Rothchild's name to the long list. I finished off my margarita and placed the glass on the miniature night table next to the bed.

"Duly noted." Garrett looked out the window and sighed. "It's a shame we're holed up in our room and missing all this beautiful scenery."

A loud knock, followed by a sharp demand to open the door, had Old Man Jenkins hoisting himself out of the swivel chair to open our cabin door.

"What are you doing in here?" Barger demanded. "I have the occupants of this sleeping car as Garrett and Ryli Kimble. I told you people to go back to your rooms and not talk about the case. And don't think I didn't already see you two ladies sneaking out going who knows where about thirty minutes ago."

Aunt Shirley snorted. "Arrest us then."

Barger's face turned red and he pointed out the door. "Get out."

CHAPTER 12

"I'm going to ask you a few questions while I search your sleeping car," Barger snapped.

I looked at Garrett to gauge his reaction. I didn't think there was any way Garrett would stand for that.

I was wrong.

Garrett shrugged and took a step back, indicating to Barger he could have the room.

What the heck?

I tried giving him my big eyes, but Garrett ignored me.

"So, the way I understand it," Barger said as he rummaged around in the top drawer of our tiny dresser, "you two lovebirds were the ones to discover the collar was missing. Is that right?"

Garrett's eyes never left Barger's hands. "There were five of us in the viewing car at the time of the discovery."

I reeled back as though hit. *Was Garrett trying to shift blame to Aunt Shirley or Old Man Jenkins? What would be the purpose of that?*

Garrett gave a small shake of his head. He obviously didn't want me asking him what he was doing, but I couldn't help but wonder what the heck he was thinking!

Barger stopped rummaging and straightened. "Five? You're saying either the Jenkins family or Mrs. Rothchild herself stole the collar?"

Garrett shrugged. "I'm saying there were five people in the viewing car. You implied Ryli and I were the only ones in the

84

viewing car when we made the discovery that the collar was missing. I was simply pointing out there were five people in the car when the discovery was made."

Barger narrowed his beady eyes at Garrett. "Don't think I don't know what you're trying to do. You think just because you're some big-time policeman that you're better than me?"

Garrett smiled condescendingly at Barger. "Not at all."

I coughed so I wouldn't laugh. I realized Garrett was trying to put Barger off. Only reason he'd do that was so he could glean information without Barger knowing.

Barger's face turned red. He took a notebook out of his pocket and read for a minute. "I just spoke with Floyd and June Hughes, and Floyd said you two were the only ones that were around Mrs. Rothchild today."

I snorted. "First off, he's been three sheets to the wind since he stepped onto this train, there's no way he could have known that or anything else for that matter. And secondly, there were plenty of people around Mrs. Rothchild today. You spoke to Mrs. Rothchild upstairs. Didn't she tell you that?"

Barger's nostrils flared. "I spoke briefly to her upstairs in the viewing room, as you well know. That's where I saw you and your aunt running into coach together."

Garrett lifted one eyebrow at me, but I just smiled and shrugged.

"Mrs. Rothchild is last on my list to interrogate fully," Barger said. "I want to interview everyone else before I get Mrs. Rothchild's take on what she believed happened. I was just gauging your reaction to my question. And I'll have you know,

Mrs. Kimble, you have failed my test." He leaned in close to me. "What are you hiding?"

My mouth dropped open. *Was this guy for real? Could he really be that bad at his job?*

I turned to Garrett. "Please tell me I wasn't this inept when I first started out?"

Garrett's mouth twitched like he was trying not to smile. "Do you forget your very first murder investigation? I'm still not one hundred percent sure what you did to Patty Carter to make her despise you still to this day."

"Oh, yeah," I mumbled.

On my first case, I'd been so sure Patty Carter was not only the killer, but she was also the person who poisoned my cat, Miss Molly. I forced Aunt Shirley, Paige, and Mindy to ride along with me as I went to terrorize and confront Patty. Long story short…Aunt Shirley ended up throwing a clay pot at Patty and knocking her out. Aunt Shirley then tied her up and pulled a gun on Patty for intimidation purposes—only to find out she wasn't the killer. It ended with Patty pulling out her even *bigger* gun and shooting at us as we tore out of her driveway in the Falcon.

"Point taken," I said. "My bad."

Garrett laughed softly. "I can assure you, Mr. Barger, that if you rely on my wife's reactions or Aunt Shirley's reactions to solve this case, you're gonna be in for a world of hurt." He paused and looked pointedly at me. "Trust me on that, Barger."

Without another word, Barger turned and strode into the bathroom. I couldn't see what he was doing, but I could hear items being moved around. A few minutes later he came back out. "This is not over. I'm convinced you and your partners, the Jenkinses, have something to do with this theft. I find it too coincidental that every time something bad happens, you two women seem to be right there."

"You'll get used to it," Garrett said. "I did."

I scowled at Garrett then turned to Barger. "Every time something bad happens? This is the first time something bad has happened. It's not considered coincidental until —"

"You know what I mean!" Barger shouted as he pointed his finger at me. "I think you two here and the Jenkinses are behind this somehow."

"Do not shout and point your finger at my wife," Garrett said quietly. I knew that voice. Barger better high-tail it out of the room fast if he wanted to live. "If that is what you really think—that we are somehow behind this theft—then all I can say is you will be spinning your wheels on us while the real thief gets away with the theft. But if that's what you think, then you better be able to prove it."

Barger frowned at Garrett's words. His pinched lips and narrow eyes left no doubt that Barger was angry… but I was unclear if it was because he couldn't prove we did the theft or because he knew we didn't but wasn't going to back down.

"Now, if you are done asking these ridiculous questions and pawing through my wife's underwear drawer," Garrett said, "I'll ask you to leave our car."

Barger's face again turned red. I was beginning to feel sorry for the fool. He obviously had no idea how to go about solving a crime.

"Do not leave this room," Barger said as he strode to our door.

"Ever?" I asked.

Barger turned and scowled at me. "You know what I mean!" He turned and slammed out of our sleeping car.

I raised my eyebrows at Garrett. "What do we do now?"

"I hate to say this, but I think we need to put our heads together and solve this case before Barger ends up letting the real thief go free."

"Do you really think Mrs. Rothchild did this?"

Garrett shrugged. "I honestly don't know. But I think it might be in our best interest—Mrs. Rothchild's included—if she pretends to personally hire us to find the collar."

My eyes lit up. "Really? You want us to talk to Mrs. Rothchild tonight about hiring us to find Muffy's collar?" My heart raced at the idea of doing a job with Garrett.

Garrett hugged me to him and kissed my head. "Looks that way." He led me over to the window and we sat down in the swivel chairs. "Now, let's enjoy this view before it's gone."

I grinned suggestively at my new husband. The lovely view I wanted to gaze at was not outside.

CHAPTER 13

"At least we still have a beautiful view for a little while longer." I zipped up my knee-high black boots over my psychedelic, butter-smooth leggings and peered out the window. It was almost time for dinner and the sun was going down on the canyon. I could barely make out the rugged ridges from the mountainside.

"I'm enjoying the view just fine." Garrett gave me a wink then pulled a blue-gray, long-sleeved shirt over his head and down his lean body.

"Is that so?" I wrapped my arms around his neck and gave him a quick kiss.

A knock drew us apart and Garrett went to open the door to Old Man Jenkins and Aunt Shirley. I took one look at Aunt Shirley and groaned.

"Why do you have that hideous dress on?" I asked. "I thought I told you to throw that thing away!"

Aunt Shirley did a little twirl in her forest green cowgirl dress. I hadn't seen the ghastly thing since we went on the murder mystery weekend for her birthday. "I knew it would be perfect for the entertainment after dinner."

"What entertainment?" Garrett asked.

"The karaoke party," Aunt Shirley said. "Didn't you read the brochure?"

Garrett laughed and shook his head. "I'm not doing karaoke."

"Me, either!" Old Man Jenkins exclaimed.

"We don't need you two spoilsports. Do we, Ryli?" Aunt Shirley slid her arm through mine, and it was all I could do not to openly weep. I didn't want to do karaoke, either.

"I bet Jenkins and I could be persuaded to watch and cheer you two on," Garrett said with a twinkle in his eye.

"You're on." Aunt Shirley turned to me. "I thought we'd start with "It's Raining Men," then move into "Tequila Makes Her Clothes Fall Off." And if there's an encore, I say we do "My Humps."

My mouth dropped open. "Um, no!"

"We'll discuss it over dinner," Aunt Shirley said as she led me out of the sleeping car.

I looked over my shoulder and glared at Garrett when I heard him and Old Man Jenkins laugh. We ascended the stairs and made our way to the dining car. I waved hello to Jack behind the lounge counter, who was busy hacking away at ice with the deadly ice pick, and ambled down the aisle to our assigned dining car.

A red-eyed Mrs. Rothchild, along with a totally oblivious Muffy, was already seated at a two-person table with Clive. The leather-warn cowboy looked to be doing his best to cheer her up. By the look on Mrs. Rothchild's face it wasn't working.

"Hello, Mrs. Rothchild," I said as we slid into a four-person table next to them. "How are you feeling?"

"Oh, dear. I wish I could say I'm doing better. But the truth is I'm not." She put her face in Muffy's neck. "I just hope this doesn't cause some sort of lasting trauma for Muffy. I was just telling Clive here I think I should take Muffy to a doggy psychiatrist when I get home."

Clive smiled gently at Mrs. Rothchild before turning to us. "I assured her she should do whatever she feels is necessary, but I'm pretty sure Muffy will be able to bounce back."

I could see the twinkle in his eyes, but I didn't think he was making fun of Mrs. Rothchild. He honestly seemed to care about her. I really hoped neither one was behind the stolen collar.

"Hey, now," Clive whistled when he caught sight of Aunt Shirley. "That's one sharp outfit you got on there."

Aunt Shirley preened. "Thank you. Ryli and I are singing karaoke tonight, and I thought it would be perfect."

It was on the tip of my tongue to tell her I wasn't singing with her, but I refrained. Sometimes practicing good manners sucked.

"Mrs. Rothchild here has agreed to be my date and accompany me to the party," Clive preened. "Isn't that right, Mrs. Rothchild?"

Mrs. Rothchild blushed. "How many times do I have to tell you to call me Eloise?"

Clive smiled slowly at Mrs. Rothchild. "Isn't that right, Eloise? You've agreed to be my date to the karaoke party?"

Mrs. Rothchild scratched Muffy's bare head and nodded enthusiastically. "I think it's just the thing Muffy and I need to take our minds off this terrible crime."

Movement caught my attention and I looked up to find Floyd and June making their way into the dining car. Floyd looked unsteady on his feet, which was nothing new. June looked like she'd been crying all afternoon, and her usual defeated look was even more prevalent tonight. She gathered her gray cardigan sweater around her body and quietly sat down at a four-person table behind Mrs. Rothchild and Clive.

Christopher ambled down the center aisle and stopped at our table to get our drinks.

The two men ordered beers while Aunt Shirley and I ordered margaritas.

"You okay?" Aunt Shirley asked Christopher. "You don't look so good."

Christopher turned so his back was to Mrs. Rothchild. "I'm just so upset over everything that has happened. Barger says he still doesn't know what happened to the diamonds."

"Waiter!" Floyd bellowed as he snapped his finger. "I need a drink."

Christopher sighed. "Excuse me. I'll be right back with your drinks and to take your order."

"I don't think any of us should be shocked Barger hasn't located the diamonds yet," Aunt Shirley said.

Garrett chuckled. "I agree."

I leaned in across the table to whisper. "Listen, Garrett thinks we should get Mrs. Rothchild to hire us to find Muffy's collar."

Aunt Shirley's eyes lit up as she stared at Garrett. "You do?"

Garrett shrugged. "I don't like the direction Barger is taking the investigation—making it seem like he's looking at us for the job. If we can convince Mrs. Rothchild to hire us, that will go a long way into having Christopher on our side. Those two are obviously close. Maybe we can use that friendship to our advantage. Make it easier for us to investigate and go places we might otherwise be barred."

Aunt Shirley let out a little whoop, and I quickly shushed her when everyone turned to stare at our table.

"I like your thinking, Ace," Aunt Shirley whispered. "We'll do it tonight when she's up with Clive singing karaoke."

Well, so much for getting out of singing.

Garrett patted my hand as though he knew what I was thinking. At least he felt my pain and could sympathize. I knew from my time spent with Aunt Shirley that karaoke wasn't going to be pretty.

We gave Christopher our order and made small talk while we waited for our food.

Harold and Angelica Walsh glided into the dining car as though they didn't have a care in the world. Harold was looking relaxed and almost human again, and Angelica looked stunning in a sexy red pantsuit with a white lace cami. Her dark hair was pulled back in a chignon, and her makeup was flawless.

I gave Harold a tight smile since he was facing me, but I couldn't help but wonder about the sudden change. Could they be more relaxed because they stole the collar and knew their money troubles were over? And was I even certain they *were* more relaxed or was it just my imagination?

"So, did that security guy find your fancy jewels?" Floyd said loudly.

Clive turned in his seat and scowled at Floyd. "Don't you think if the diamonds had been found we'd be celebrating? Show some manners."

Floyd's face turned red and he started to rise from his seat. "I'll show you manners. Get up and we'll settle this like men."

Clive made a move to get up.

Old Man Jenkins caught Garrett's eye.

Garrett slid out of his seat and stood in the middle of the aisle looking at both men. "You both are going to sit down right now." Garrett slid his hands in his pockets as though he were calm. But I knew from his set jaw he was pretty wound.

Mrs. Rothchild let out a small cry, and Muffy immediately set to licking Mrs. Rothchild's neck in comfort. I couldn't gauge June's or Angelica's reaction because their backs were to me, but everyone else looked relieved that Garrett had finally stepped in.

Floyd's eyes darkened and he puffed out his chest. "How dare you speak to me like that. I don't know who you think you are, but you have no right to—"

Christopher walked in from the kitchen carrying two trays of food. He stopped short when he saw the confrontation.

"Is something wrong?" Christopher asked nervously.

No one said a word. Garrett continued to stare at Floyd until Floyd lowered his eyes and sat back down in his seat.

"Nothing's wrong," Garrett said. "Everything's fine."

Garrett slid back down in his chair, and I wrapped my hand around his. Christopher took Harold and Angelica's dinner order, and I tried my best to ignore Floyd's icy glare the rest of the meal.

CHAPTER 14

After dinner June and Floyd went back to their room. Surprisingly, Harold and Angelica agreed to accompany the rest of us up to the lounge car in section C that was hosting the karaoke party.

"I've never been to a karaoke party," Angelica said primly.

I can't say I was surprised. She didn't look the type.

"You'll love it," Aunt Shirley assured her as we all strode through the viewing car and past our staircase to yank open the doors that would lead to coach. There were a few people still milling around in coach, but it looked like most had opted to attend the karaoke party.

We made our way into the next car, which was the lounge in section C where the party was happening. This car looked just like the lounge we had for our personal use. I waved to Jack who was serving drinks behind the counter with another man. He gave me a head nod and smiled.

The lounge was jam packed with people. You could hardly move without bumping into someone. This was so not my idea of a good time. I really just wanted to go back downstairs and spend quality time with Garrett.

Christopher waved to us from across the lounge. He handed two more drinks off to people before pushing his way over to us.

"Mrs. Rothchild, it's nice to see you participating in karaoke night," Christopher said. "I don't think I've ever seen you over here on karaoke nights before."

Mrs. Rothchild chuckled. "I admit this isn't my usual scene, but it sounded like fun."

"Well, I'm working all night until the party ends at midnight," Christopher said. "So if you need anything, let me know."

Christopher dug into his pocket and gave Muffy a dog bone before heading back out to serve.

"You men go get us some drinks while we find the book that has songs in it," Aunt Shirley said.

Ten minutes later the four of us girls were huddled together pouring over song choices.

"We're not singing "Baby Got Back" or "I Wanna Sex You Up" tonight," I said exasperatingly to Aunt Shirley. I was about to lose my ever-loving mind and whack her a good one.

"Don't be such a prude," Aunt Shirley said. "Everyone likes these songs."

"No one likes them," I gritted out between clenched teeth.

Mrs. Rothchild giggled and drew Muffy close to her chest. "There are some pretty risqué songs in this booklet."

Aunt Shirley tapped her finger repeatedly on the paper. "How about this one?"

I leaned down to see the title and laughed. "You ain't no Fergie."

"This Fergie singing about her humps," Mrs. Rothchild said, "are they what I think they are?"

Angelica let out a soft giggle before catching herself. "I really don't know any of these songs, either. Maybe I should just sit this out and watch you three ladies."

"No way," I said. "If I have to be tortured, so do you!"

96

Plus, I need to start questioning you as to where you were at the time of the robbery.

"Fine," Aunt Shirley huffed. "How about "It's Raining Men" then? Everyone loves that song, and it should be tame enough for you."

I knew arguing would be futile, so I nodded my head and prayed we'd be so far down on the list we wouldn't have time to perform.

Garrett saddled up next to me. "Here ya go." He handed me a margarita, and I downed half the glass. "Whoa!"

I gave him an exasperated look. "I just vetoed the most suggestive songs you can imagine. I deserve a drink to get through this night."

Garrett threw back his head and laughed. "You're right."

"So did Barger come to your sleeping car today and ask you about the robbery?" Aunt Shirley asked Angelica and Harold.

Nothing like jumping in with two feet.

Angelica shot Harold a look before she answered. "Yes. He searched our room and then asked us questions like we were common criminals. I'm thinking about filing a complaint with the railroad about my treatment."

Harold sighed. "He was just doing his job, Angelica."

"Since when is accusing a law-abiding citizen of theft acceptable behavior?" Angelica hissed back.

"I'm sorry," Mrs. Rothchild said as she stroked Muffy's back. "This is all my fault. I never thought something like this could happen."

I decided to steer the conversation more toward Angelica being the hero since she was so put out. "Could you give Barger any information? I mean, you were the first to leave the dining car. Did you notice anyone in the viewing car when you left?"

Angelica sniffed. "I'll tell you the same thing I told that Barger person…when I walked through the viewing car, the people I saw were Clive, Mrs. Rothchild, and June."

My mouth dropped. "You saw June? As in June Hughes?"

Angelica nodded. "Yes. She was asking Clive if Christopher was around. She had a headache and needed pain reliever."

Clive nodded. "That's right. I told June I thought Christopher was in coach."

That jells with Aunt Shirley saying Christopher was running back and forth between the cars.

I turned to Aunt Shirley. "When you entered the lounge car this morning, it was about five minutes after Angelica left. Who was left in the viewing car when you and Old Man Jenkins went through?"

Aunt Shirley pursed her lips. "No one. Mrs. Rothchild was sleeping alone in the viewing car."

I turned back to Clive. "Where were you? You were supposed to stay with Mrs. Rothchild."

Clive flushed. "I got an important text from my friend who's buying my cows. So I excused myself to call him."

"Where was June?" Aunt Shirley asked.

Clive shrugged. "Just standing there by the landing. She looked pretty out of it. I think she said something about looking for Christopher in coach, but I had already started down the stairs to make my phone call."

Mrs. Rothchild nodded her head. "That's right. I remember seeing June now. I must have drifted off to sleep when she went to look for Christopher."

"Did you notice if Muffy had her collar on when you were making your way to the lounge?" I asked Aunt Shirley and Old Man Jenkins.

They both shook their heads.

"I didn't look," Aunt Shirley said.

"Me, either," Old Man Jenkins added.

I turned to Harold. "When you left the lounge, who all was in the viewing car?"

Harold looked uncomfortable. "No one. Just Mrs. Rothchild. She was asleep, so I kept on walking."

Did you?

"And don't forget about Floyd," Aunt Shirley said. "He would have been alone with her, too."

"I didn't do anything wrong!" Harold exclaimed.

"No one said you did," I assured him. "I'm just trying to look closer at the timeline. But you're right, Aunt Shirley. Floyd left the lounge after Harold, so he would have been alone with her for a few minutes, also."

"But don't you think Muffy would have barked if someone like Floyd had gotten close to her?" Mrs. Rothchild asked as she gave Muffy a hug.

I didn't want to hurt Mrs. Rothchild's feelings by telling her maybe Muffy wasn't exactly the best watch dog in the world.

"Not necessarily," Garrett said smoothly. "I don't think we should take Floyd off the table just because Muffy didn't bark."

"How long did your phone call take?" I asked Clive.

Clive looked down and shuffled his boots. "I thought the phone call would only take a few minutes, but it ended up taking about thirty. By the time I hung up, I found out from the others that Eloise and Muffy had been robbed."

I looked over at Christopher. He was busy handing out drinks and chatting up the ladies. Could Christopher have sneaked back into the viewing lounge after everyone had left and snagged the collar?

As far as I was concerned, Christopher, June, Harold, and Floyd had moved up to the top of my suspect list.

CHAPTER 15

The DJ took the mic and opened the night with a pulse-beating jam. I had no idea what it was, but it got everyone excited. A few people danced where they were, while others sang along. As I scanned the crowd, I caught the eye of a well-dressed man in his early forties, short brown hair, hazel eyes, and a decent body. He shifted his gaze to Aunt Shirley, lifted his drink in a salute, and grinned.

"You know him?" I asked Aunt Shirley.

Old Man Jenkins scoffed. "Leave it to your aunt to find the one single guy in coach this morning to flirt with."

"Oh hush!" Aunt Shirley said exasperatingly. Although I could tell she was quite pleased with herself. "You're just jealous."

The handsome man slowly made his way through the crowd until he was standing next to us. Another singer was called to the stage and the music began to play. It only took a few words into the song before I wished I had a saw to hack off my ears. Tone deaf didn't do her justice.

"Hi." He gave us all a wide, friendly smile which showed off his dimples. "Aunt Shirley, right?"

"You got it, sonny. What was your name again?"

"Kevin Wilson."

"Well Kevin Wilson," Aunt Shirley said, "you like to sing?"

Kevin took a small step back and shook his head. "Nope. Not me. I'm just here to watch."

"Did you get on at Kansas City or Denver?" I asked.

"Denver. I'm actually heading to Oklahoma City."

"Business?" I asked.

He gave me a serious look before shrugging. "You can say that."

Another cryptic passenger. Just what this train ride needed.

"What about you folks?" Kevin asked amiably. "I know from talking to Aunt Shirley this morning that she's on her honeymoon, but what about the rest of you?"

I looked surreptitiously at Garrett. I wasn't sure what it was about Kevin Wilson that struck me as a little...off. He was a little too friendly. A little too curious.

"Business." Harold wrapped his arm around his wife. Angelica stiffened and shrugged Harold's arm off her.

"Same," Clive said. "Headed to Oklahoma City on business."

Mrs. Rothchild looked at Clive and smiled. "Well, Muffy and I are just riding the rails looking for a good time."

"And you two?" Kevin asked Garrett.

Garrett said nothing for a few seconds. "Honeymoon, also. Aunt Shirley is Ryli's great-aunt."

Kevin laughed and looked at me. "Really? That must be one wild ride."

Geez, what had Aunt Shirley told this guy?

"You can say that," I said, giving his words a few minutes ago right back to him.

No one said anything for a few seconds, just taking in the energy of the room. The song finally finished, and the tone-deaf singer took a bow to whistles and applause.

The DJ thanked the tone-deaf girl and introduced the next singer. "Up next, we have Sissy and Mike singing a duet from *Grease*."

More applause and whistles as the song came blaring out over the speakers.

"So," Kevin said once the noise had died down, "I hear there was a little bit of a commotion with a theft in your area this morning."

"You heard about that?" Garrett asked.

Kevin looked Garrett in the eye. "Yes. I was just wondering how the investigation was going? Have you heard anything new?"

"Is there a particular reason why you're interested?" Garrett asked.

The tension was so thick you could cut it with a knife. Music and noise reverberated around us, but the nine of us stood silently together, measuring each other.

"You could say that," Kevin finally said. "Not really my jurisdiction, but I'm always curious when things happen."

I looked sharply at Kevin.

Jurisdiction? Was he a cop, too?

Mrs. Rothchild sniffed and hugged Muffy close to her. "My poor little Muffy was robbed."

"You know," Angelica said suddenly, "I'm not feeling well. Harold, I think we need to go to our room. I need to lie down. All this loud music is giving me a migraine."

"Don't be silly," Aunt Shirley said. "We should be going on any minute."

Angelica shot her husband a look that should have had him bursting into flames.

"Right. Of course." Harold finished his drink and set it on the table behind him. "Loud noises usually don't sit well with Angelica. We better head back to our room. It was nice talking with everyone tonight."

The two excused themselves and strode out of the room and into the coach section of the train.

"Well, that was a fast retreat," Aunt Shirley grumbled.

"Sure was," Old Man Jenkins agreed.

Maybe I need to put both Harold and Angelica on that list of immediate suspects. She did threaten he better come up with a plan to get some money quick or she was gone.

"What kind of law enforcement?" Garrett asked.

Kevin gave a small smile. "FBI. You?"

"Chief of Police in my town of Granville."

Agent Wilson shook Garrett's hand. "I thought I recognized a fellow brother."

"Why didn't you tell me this morning you were FBI?" Aunt Shirley demanded.

Agent Wilson chuckled. "Well, I really didn't get much of a chance to talk. Not that I'm complaining," he said hurriedly when he saw the look on Aunt Shirley's face. "I enjoyed listening to you and your stories. Besides, telling people I'm in the FBI isn't something I usually open with."

"Maybe you can help Mrs. Rothchild get her collar back," Clive suggested.

A look of pain crossed Agent Wilson's face. "Like I said before, it's not really my jurisdiction. If a federal crime is committed, I'm your guy. But I just can't assume my way into an investigation simply because of a theft." He turned to Mrs.

Rothchild. "I'm sorry to hear about you and Muffy getting robbed. Believe me, if I could take over this investigation, I would."

"Maybe now's a good time to discuss that," Aunt Shirley said.

Garrett nodded.

"As you know, Eloise," Aunt Shirley said, "Garrett is a policeman. I was a private investigator for more decades than I can count, and Ryli here is taking her investigator's test when we get home. I've spent a year training her. The three of us are a pretty good team, so we'd like to offer you our services. If you want, we can snoop around for you and see what we find out."

Mrs. Rothchild's eyes filled with tears. "Would you really?" She buried her head in Muffy's neck. "Muffy and I would love nothing more than for you guys to help out. How much would you charge?"

"Nothing," Garrett said quickly.

Aunt Shirley opened her mouth to argue, but Garrett cut her off again.

"We aren't going to charge you for our services," Garrett said. "We just want to help."

Mrs. Rothchild leaned forward and rested her silver head against Garrett's arm. "You're a good man."

Garrett looked a little panicked, but he lifted his free hand to pat Mrs. Rothchild on the head.

"And if you can put in a good word to Christopher for us," I said, "that would be great. If he knows we're wanting to help you, maybe he can let us know where Barger is in the investigation. Or something like that."

"Of course," Mrs. Rothchild said. "I know Christopher would be glad to help out however he can."

"That's awful nice of you folks," Clive said. "Eloise has been so worried."

"And I'll do my part listening and gathering any clues I can from coach," Agent Wilson said. "I'm sorry I can't help out more, but it's really not my place."

"I understand," Mrs. Rothchild said. "And I feel so relieved knowing you guys will help Muffy get her collar back."

The DJ's voice came barreling out of the speakers once again. "And now, put your hands together for Aunt Shirley and the Temples!"

CHAPTER 16

I groaned at the ridiculous name. I barely had time to thrust my drink at Garrett before Aunt Shirley pulled Mrs. Rothchild and me up to the platform area…Muffy yipping in excitement. The DJ handed us each a microphone and started the music.

"You ladies ready for a shower?" Aunt Shirley hollered into the mic. "Because it's raining men!"

Screams and shouts went up and Aunt Shirley and Mrs. Rothchild started singing the first line of the song. I looked out at Garrett, who was grinning like an idiot. He motioned for me to sing, and I narrowed my eyes at him.

Aunt Shirley must have realized I wasn't singing because she slapped me on my arm. I staggered to the side of the platform but caught myself before I fell. Luckily it was time for the chorus. I knew that part. Glancing over at Mrs. Rothchild, I couldn't help but smile. She was singing Hallelujah to Muffy about it raining men. Getting into the spirit, I raised the mic up to my mouth and followed the words on the screen.

Not to be outdone, Aunt Shirley stepped forward and did a little impromptu dance tease. She thrust her arms out wide, still bellowing the lyrics, and shimmied and shook as the crowd screamed. The tassels on her cowgirl dress were swaying provocatively in all directions.

Old Man Jenkins was shaking his head and grinning at Aunt Shirley. Not for the first time did I wonder if that man truly knew what he'd gotten himself into when he married Aunt Shirley.

Luckily the song ended, and I handed my mic back to the DJ. I was helping Aunt Shirley and Mrs. Rothchild off the platform when the odious DJ asked, "Did you guys enjoy that?"

Screams and cat whistles went up again.

"How about an encore?" The DJ asked. "I hear Aunt Shirley does a great rendition of "Tequila Makes Her Clothes Fall Off."

Aunt Shirley grinned and grabbed a microphone back from the DJ. "I need a shot! Who's buying me a round?"

Two different men standing around the bar ordered shots at the same time. Shaking my head, Mrs. Rothchild and I slowly made our way back to the guys. I didn't want to make any sudden moves in case Aunt Shirley saw me and made me go back on stage with her. No way was I singing that song in front of a bunch of strangers.

The tequila shots reached Aunt Shirley and she grabbed the first one and downed it. Whistles and cat calls exploded in the lounge car again. I put my hands over my ears. It felt like my eardrums were about to shatter.

Garrett leaned down to my ear and removed one of my hands. "Your aunt knows how to command a crowd, I'll give her that."

Aunt Shirley grabbed the other shot and took it with her back on stage. She set the drink on the stand and began singing and dancing to going out with her friends and drinking tequila and losing items of clothing. When an instrumental part came on, Aunt Shirley reached over and downed the other shot. She then kicked off her shoes and undid the top two buttons on her cowgirl dress. Once again her tassels were flying high and her boobs were hanging low. When the song mentioned taking off her nylons, my heart stopped at the thought of Aunt Shirley doing just that. Luckily someone in the crowd handed her another shot and she put her dress down and tossed back the drink. Lobbing the empty shot glass back at the guy, Aunt Shirley staggered back to the stage to strut her stuff. It didn't help that the video behind her was currently showing a naked grandma with black strips across all her girlie bits jumping into a swimming pool full of young people.

By the time the song was finished, there wasn't a single person not screaming or whistling. Even Garrett and Old Man Jenkins were into the show. I caught Agent Wilson's eye again and he grinned and whistled once more before taking a drink of his beer.

"She's some lady," Agent Wilson yelled over the crowd.

"She sure is," Old Man Jenkins said with so much love in his voice tears stung my eyes.

Aunt Shirley came running over to us, fanning herself and preening at the back slaps and applause. "Whew! I'm hotter than Satan's housecat. Someone get me some water, would ya?"

"Thank you for not taking all your clothes off," I said dryly.

Aunt Shirley grinned. "I thought about it." She pointed to Garrett. "But I was afraid Ace here would arrest me for indecent exposure."

Garrett's lips twitched. "Make no mistake about it. I'd have had you handcuffed before you had your dress completely unbuttoned."

"Spoil sport!" Aunt Shirley pouted.

"I found it a very lively rendition of the original song," Agent Wilson said with a twinkle in his eye.

Aunt Shirley winked at him. "You're all right for an FBI guy."

Agent Wilson blushed.

"Well," Mrs. Rothchild said, "Muffy and I have had a wonderful time tonight. Thank you all so much for taking my mind off the robbery. I can't tell you how much that means to me and Muffy."

"You do look happier," Clive said.

"Speaking of the robbery," Garrett said. "Has anyone spoken to Barger since he finished searching and questioning everyone?"

We all shook our heads.

"I bet he's sweating bullets calling in for help at the head office," Aunt Shirley cackled.

As if on cue, Barger swaggered into the lounge, hands on his hips, gun showing. He stood by a crowded table and surveyed the room. When his eyes fell on us, he scowled. Pushing and shoving others out of his way, he came over to where we were standing.

"Well, well," Barger drawled. "If this don't look suspicious."

"Suspicious how, you ninny?" Aunt Shirley demanded.

Barger's face turned red. "Watch how you're addressing me. I'd hate to have to take you to the train's holding cell."

Aunt Shirley laughed. "For what? Name calling?"

"For insulting a police officer," Barger bellowed.

"First off," Agent Wilson said, "that's not a punishable offense."

"You tell him," Old Man Jenkins said, giving Barger the evil eye.

"And second," Garrett chimed in behind Agent Wilson, "the fact we're all standing here is not suspicious. We're here attending the karaoke party the train is throwing. Just like everyone else in this room."

"Who're you?" Barger asked Agent Wilson, ignoring Garrett.

"FBI Agent Kevin Wilson. Who are you?"

Barger's eyes bulged. "We got FBI on the train? Why wasn't I informed about all the extra law enforcement?"

Agent Wilson shrugged. "Because there's no reason to let you know. I'm just making my way to Oklahoma City's FBI field office."

"I don't like this," Barger muttered. "This is my train. I have this robbery under control. I should have an arrest by tomorrow afternoon. So I don't need FBI poking their nose into this."

Agent Wilson held up his hands. "I'm not poking my nose in anywhere."

Barger tossed back his shoulders as he sauntered off.

"Yet," Agent Wilson muttered.

CHAPTER 17

I groaned and rolled over onto my back. My head was pounding and my tongue was stuck to the roof of my mouth. I willed my stomach to stop rolling and opened one eye. Then promptly shut it.

Mrs. Rothchild and Clive stayed up until ten before turning in for the night, while the rest of us went to our viewing car for privacy and talked more about the missing diamonds. And have a few more drinks thanks to Aunt Shirley.

I was glad Agent Wilson had opted to join us. Another professional on the job, without really being on the job, would definitely be a help. By the time we parted company, it was around eleven, and we were about two hours outside of Albuquerque, the next stop on our trip.

"You doing okay there, Sin?" Garrett asked.

"No. I hate that woman. I always say I'm just going to go for a little while…have one drink. Next thing I know I'm hungover, sporting a tattoo, and have no memory of the previous night."

Garrett laughed softly. "Trust me, you didn't get a tattoo."

"Well, my body is in a lot of pain, so I just assumed."

Garrett laughed again. "You're one in a million, Sin."

I stuck my tongue out at him.

"That tongue looks rough," Garrett said as he rolled out of the bed. "You need some water."

"And pain reliever. My head is pounding."

"You got it."

He padded over to the mini fridge and took out a tiny water. Struggling, I managed to sit up and wondered if it was the train or my insides that were rumbling. "Here." Garrett tossed the bottle of water to me. Unfortunately, I have no coordination. The water hit me in the center of my chest and fell in my lap.

"Geez," Garrett said, shaking his head, "you're gonna have to work out and get your body moving if you want to chase bad guys for a living."

I scowled at him. "Okay, *Hank.* Thanks for the pep talk."

Garrett shrugged. "Hank's right."

He turned and walked into the bathroom, leaving me alone to wrestle with the pain reliever on my nightstand. If I didn't know deep down inside that Hank was right, I'd walk in that bathroom and give Garrett a piece of my mind. As it was, I elected to stay in bed and recuperate.

"You awake?" Garrett asked as he kissed my forehead.

I opened my eyes and groaned. I must have fallen back asleep.

"I'm awake," I mumbled.

Garrett was dressed in jeans and t-shirt. I looked over at the clock and was shocked to see it was after nine.

"We're gonna be late for breakfast." Not that I wanted any, but we were supposed to meet Aunt Shirley and Old Man Jenkins.

"Don't worry," Garrett chuckled. "I texted Jenkins a while ago and he said Aunt Shirley is slow moving this morning."

I didn't even bother hiding my evil smile. I was kinda glad she was getting a taste of her own medicine.

"But I could use some runny eggs and bacon," Garrett grinned.

"You're a vile man," I groaned.

"C'mon. Let's get you in the shower." Garrett pulled me up by my arms and tossed back my bedsheet. Helping me to my feet, he lifted my nightgown off my body.

"Don't even think of getting frisky," I mumbled.

Garrett chuckled as he led me to the bathroom. "Wouldn't dream of it, Sin."

Fifteen minutes later I was dressed in a pair of jeans and t-shirt, my hair pulled up in a high ponytail, and my face free of last night's makeup. I slipped my feet into a pair of black slip-ons and followed Garrett into the dining car.

It was virtually empty.

Aunt Shirley, Old Man Jenkins, and Agent Wilson sat at a table.

"Where is everyone?" I asked as we slid in next to them at a two-person table.

"You just missed Clive and Mrs. Rothchild," Aunt Shirley said. "Mrs. Rothchild is worried because she can't find Christopher. I guess he usually knocks on her door and makes sure she's up by seven every morning. He didn't this morning, and so she and Clive have gone off to find him."

I frowned. "I remember seeing him last night still in the lounge when we all left."

"That party ended around midnight," Agent Wilson said. "I could still hear the music and noise from coach when I tried to go to sleep around eleven-fifteen."

I looked out the window. "So we're in Texas heading to Oklahoma City?"

"Yep," Agent Wilson said. "I believe we pulled out of Albuquerque around three this morning."

"What can I get you?" Jack asked as he stopped by our table.

"What're you doing here?" I asked in surprise.

"I got a text from Christopher last night around one-thirty. He said he wasn't feeling well and asked me to fill in for him this morning."

"Well, someone needs to tell Mrs. Rothchild," I said. "Seems she's been fretting about him all morning."

Jack frowned. "She didn't say anything to me this morning about being worried. I'll make sure she knows he's under the weather."

"He didn't look sick last night," Aunt Shirley mused.

Jack smiled. "He might have indulged a little too much. It wouldn't be the first time I've covered for Christopher over the years."

"I'll take two eggs over easy, four slices of bacon, and whole-wheat toast," Garrett said.

I opted for a greasy cheeseburger.

"Cheeseburger for breakfast?" Garrett asked.

"That's right," I said, staring him in the eye.

"What kind of woman did I marry?" Garrett joked.

"One that eats cheeseburgers for breakfast," I countered back.

Jack laughed and jotted down our orders. "Be right back with your food."

Jack took off toward the kitchen and I poured a cup of coffee from the carafe at our table.

Aunt Shirley stirred her coffee then took a sip. "Seems pretty quiet this morning after a rocking night last night," Aunt Shirley mused. "Anyone seen the others in our party?"

I shook my head. "No one in the viewing room."

Aunt Shirley frowned. "That seems weird."

We made small talk for a few more minutes until our food arrived. I was relieved to see a big, greasy cheeseburger placed in front of me. I'd just taken a huge bite of my manna from heaven when Mrs. Rothchild came rushing into the dinging car, Muffy in her arms, Clive close behind.

"I'm worried about Christopher," Mrs. Rothchild said.

"I've tried to calm her fears," Clive said. "But she said it's not like him to miss work like this."

I held up my hand. "Jack was telling us he got a text from Christopher around one-thirty this morning stating he wasn't feeling well. He's probably holed up in his room sick."

Mrs. Rothchild chewed on her lower lip. "I suppose. I just wish he'd answer his door."

"If you want," Aunt Shirley volunteered, "after we finish eating, Ryli and I will try rousing him."

"Oh, thank you!" Mrs. Rothchild said.

"What are we going to do that they can't?" I asked.

Aunt Shirley sent me a silent look. I knew better than to argue.

"I think Eloise and I are going to go retire in the viewing car," Clive said with a wink to Mrs. Rothchild. "Take in the beauty."

Mrs. Rothchild tittered and pulled Muffy close to her.

Clive led her out of the dining car, leaving us alone.

"Is anyone else weirded out by that whole thing?" I asked. "I mean, isn't it a little odd that Clive's on this train because he's in dire straits and needs money, and now he's attached to Mrs. Rothchild?"

"I like to think I'm a pretty good judge of character," Aunt Shirley said. "I think we all know he's sniffing around her because she has money. But I'm also willing to bet Mrs. Rothchild knows it and is perfectly okay with it."

"I pretty much said the same thing to her," Garrett said.

"But do you really think so?" I asked.

Garrett laid his hand over mine. "Yesterday when it looked like he was getting pretty cozy with her after the collar was stolen, I called Matt and had him run Clive through the system. He's clean."

I breathed a sigh of relief. "Good. I just don't want to see Mrs. Rothchild hurt."

"Let's go see if we can't rouse Christopher," Aunt Shirley said. "What are you men going to do?"

Garrett looked at Old Man Jenkins and Agent Wilson. "I think we'll head to the viewing car, too. Talk a little man talk."

I snickered and gave him a peck on the cheek. "We'll catch up with you later."

I followed Aunt Shirley out of the dining car, through the lounge, and into the viewing car. We waved to Mrs. Rothchild and Clive and descended the staircase to our sleeping cars.

"Why did you give me that crazy look?" I asked Aunt Shirley once we were alone.

"I'm hoping we can catch Christopher in a weak moment and drill him on everything he knows about the theft. He's in and out of these cars, waiting on us. Maybe he's seen something that he doesn't realize."

We stepped into the sleeping car hallway and stopped at the first door. Aunt Shirley put her ear against the door then shook her head. She knocked three times and waited.

Nothing.

CHAPTER 18

Two doors down a door opened and Harold poked his head out. "Angelica is still trying to recover from her migraine. I'd appreciate it if you people would stop pounding on the porter's door. And why is everyone pounding on his door anyway? He's obviously not there."

"We're just checking up on him and making sure he's okay," I said. "Who else has come by?"

"Clive and Mrs. Rothchild," he said. "They come by like every ten minutes. It's getting annoying."

I frowned and looked at Aunt Shirley. Surely Christopher couldn't sleep through all that ruckus?

We thanked Harold for the information and assured him we wouldn't disturb him or his wife anymore. The minute he closed the door, I whirled to face Aunt Shirley.

"What do you think?" I asked.

"I think maybe Christopher imbibed a little too much last night and is still knocked out cold."

Aunt Shirley dug around in her purse and pulled out her handy pick-a-lock contraption. Giving me a grin, she turned back to the door and jiggled the pick inside the knob. A few seconds later I heard a pop.

Aunt Shirley put her finger up to her lips. "Shh. We don't want to wake him. This could be our opportunity to snoop and see what we can find out about the robbery."

I wasn't sure how we were going to do that, but I nodded my head dutifully. I couldn't count the number of times Aunt Shirley managed to pull something useful out of her hind end during one of our stakeouts or B&Es.

We looked over our shoulders then quietly crept into the sleeping car. Christopher's room was exactly like mine, just flipped. One quick glance told us no one was in the bed…or in the car for that matter.

"He must be in the bathroom," Aunt Shirley whispered.

I crinkled my nose. The bathroom door was closed. If Christopher was really sick, I didn't want to bother him.

"Maybe we should just come back later," I hissed, moving toward the main door.

"Just give me a minute." Aunt Shirley tiptoed to the bathroom door and put her ear against the wood. "I don't hear anything."

"Gross. Let's leave the guy in peace."

Aunt Shirley knocked softly on the bathroom door.

"Christopher? It's Shirley Andr—Shirley Jenkins." I heard the resignation in Aunt Shirley's voice and had to smile. She still couldn't get used to saying her married name. "Are you okay in there?"

Silence.

Aunt Shirley knocked a little harder.

"Christopher?"

Silence.

"Oh crap," I said. "You don't suppose something bad has happened to him?"

"Only one way to find out."

Aunt Shirley grabbed hold of the door knob and swung the door open. There in the bathroom on the tile floor was a sprawled

Christopher. I peeked around Aunt Shirley to get a better view and whimpered. One side of Christopher's head had been bashed in. Blood was splattered around the floor and onto the toilet.

I put my hand over my mouth to keep from gagging.

"Keep it together," Aunt Shirley snapped. "We need to gather clues before Mrs. Rothchild and Clive come back."

"We need to notify Garrett that there's been a murder."

"In a minute. Now, let's think. Why would Christopher be murdered in the bathroom and not in his bed? Why chance someone hearing him fall?"

I took three deep breaths. "Well, Mrs. Rothchild is next door. It's not like she's going to really hear a lot. She's an elderly lady who wears hearing aids."

"And it looks like it's only one hit to the side of the head," Aunt Shirley said. "So it's not like he was beaten repeatedly upside the head by something. Probably just one good smack and down he went."

"So he probably didn't make a lot of sound," I said.

"We need to find the murder weapon," Aunt Shirley said.

I didn't say anything because at this point I couldn't care less if we found the murder weapon. "There must be something important about the bathroom since this is where his body is."

Aunt Shirley looked around the cramped room.

"I don't see anything that jumps out at me as being out of place." Aunt Shirley stood and tiptoed one step around the blood and stood at the small sink. It was lined with toothpaste, toothbrush, a razor, and deodorant. Nothing unusual.

I straightened and stepped over the body toward the shower stall. I wrapped my hand around the bottom of my t-shirt and pulled open the shower stall. "Oh, boy! I've found the murder weapon."

"What is it?"

I looked down at the bloodied fire extinguisher. "Remember the fire extinguisher that was at the end of the hall near the stairs. I'm assuming if we went out to look, it wouldn't be there."

Aunt Shirley whistled. "Beat to death with a fire extinguisher. That's a new one."

I closed the shower door and turned to face Aunt Shirley when something caught my eye…in the toilet.

Without leaving my spot in the cramped room, I leaned over as far as I could and peered down into the porcelain bowl. I wasn't certain, but it looked like something was caught in between the side and bottom of the bowl. Something round and tiny.

"I don't know if this means anything," I said. "But I think there's something caught in the bottom of the toilet."

Aunt Shirley's forehead wrinkled…even more than it naturally was.

"What do you mean there's something in there?" Aunt Shirley demanded.

"I don't know. But I'm not sticking my hand down in there and getting it!"

"Oh, yes you are."

My mouth dropped open. "The heck I am! These toilets scare me as it is. I'm not purposely putting my hand down in a toilet bowl so you can see if there's a clue in there or not! You want to find out, *you* stick your hand down there!"

"This will be good practice for when you have your own kids and have to change a diaper," Aunt Shirley argued. "Now, get your hands down in that toilet water and feel around."

I literally gagged.

"For pity sake!" Aunt Shirley growled. "Lean back and let me see what you're even talking about."

I leaned back and let Aunt Shirley peer into the toilet. "Hmm. I think you're right. It looks like a metal chain of some sort."

I took several deep breaths. "Maybe Christopher came in here to flush it down the toilet when he was attacked and murdered, but it didn't get all the way down."

Aunt Shirley squatted down next to the toilet, careful not to touch the body, and reached down into the bowl.

"Oh, gross!" I squealed.

"Hush up and push down this lever. These dang toilets have enough force to suck a person clear down."

"I know," I said. "I'm terrified of it."

"I'll grab hold of the loop with two hands, you gently ease the bottom open just a fraction of an inch. Don't open it all the way or I may not be able to hold on."

"I can't believe you're sticking your hand in another person's toilet," I grumbled. "That's the most disgusting thing I think I've ever seen you do. And I've seen you do some pretty nasty things."

"Quit your whining. Are you ready?"

"Hold on." I placed my right foot on the lever and leaned my arms forward against the wall and peered down between my arms so I could judge how far the bottom would open. Very carefully I pressed down a fraction of an inch until the bottom panel moved a tiny bit.

With a vicious yank, Aunt Shirley pulled the metal chain up from the toilet.

Toilet water flew off the metal chain and hit me square in the face. Gagging and screaming, I reeled backward and swiped at my face. Unfortunately, I tripped over Christopher's body and went down like a ton of bricks, cracking my head against the wall. Stars danced in front of my eyes, so I squeezed them shut. I also tried to ignore the fact I was now sprawled over the top of a dead man's legs.

"Well, Grace," Aunt Shirley snickered, "that was entertaining."

I didn't say anything. Not because I had better manners, but I was afraid if I opened my mouth I'd yak all over the floor.

"But on the bright side," Aunt Shirley went on, "it looks like we found the collar!"

"What?" I sat up straight and opened my eyes. Big mistake. The room spun and the cheeseburger I'd recently eaten decided it wanted to leave my body. I barely had time to turn my head before I heaved all over the threshold of the bathroom.

"How did you get to be such a pansy?" Aunt Shirley asked.

CHAPTER 19

After I'd stopped vomiting, Aunt Shirley said she'd go get help. But not before she slipped the chained collar inside her polyester pants pocket with a threat to my life if I told anyone.

"But why would Christopher flush the jewels?" I moaned. "It makes no sense."

Aunt Shirley shook her head. "I honestly don't know. I admit that move has me stumped."

"Whatever," I mumbled. "We can figure it out later. Go get Garrett to secure the body."

Only it wasn't Garrett that came to secure the body…it was Barger. And now the little weasel wouldn't stop hounding me about how we'd discovered the body.

"And so I'm supposed to just believe you two accidentally stumbled across Christopher's body in his personal bathroom?" Barger sneered.

"Get her upstairs in the viewing car, please." I looked up to see Agent Wilson standing in the doorway of Christopher's room. He gave me a small smile.

"Excuse me?" Barger snarled. "Who do you think you are coming in here on my watch, telling me how to run my investigation?"

Agent Wilson gave a small laugh. "FBI. Not only do we have a theft of diamonds, but we now have a body. I've called the Oklahoma City FBI field office, and I've been given the go-ahead to work this case. If you don't believe me, feel free to call yourself."

Barger's face turned three different shades of color. It should have given me pleasure, but I was still too woozy. "Chief Kimble, please escort your wife upstairs."

Garrett entered the room and helped me to my feet. "I should have known you'd somehow manage to stumble over a body. And this time quite literally."

I waited for the anger and lecture…but it never came. In fact, he sounded amused.

"Are you mad?" I asked as Agent Wilson moved aside to let us leave.

"At myself. I didn't see this coming." Garrett eased me out of his arms, and I carefully made my way upstairs into the viewing car. "I honestly thought you and Aunt Shirley would put your heads together and figure out who stole the diamonds, and you'd have your little adventure while I could watch over you. Keep you safe."

I laughed softly. "Jokes on you. I can't go anywhere without running into major trouble."

"Don't I know it," Garrett grumbled. "I'm sorry I wasn't there for you."

I stopped at the top of the stairs and turned to him. I gathered his face in my hands. I was about to give him a kiss when I remembered I'd just lost my breakfast all over the floor downstairs. "Garrett, you are always here for me. I always feel safe when you're around."

He smiled and kissed my forehead. "Thanks, Sin. Now, let's go see how everyone is doing."

A sobbing Mrs. Rothchild was huddled on one of the loveseats, Muffy and Clive trying their best to sooth her. Harold and Angelica paced back and forth near the doors that led to the private lounge. Floyd was nursing a drink while June sat stiffly in a chair, not looking at anyone. Aunt Shirley and Old Man Jenkins were kicked back in lounging chairs, as though they didn't have a care in the world.

The door to the lounge car opened and Jack came out carrying a couple of iced teas. He set the tray down on an empty table by Aunt Shirley, then made his way over to Mrs. Rothchild.

"Your hot tea is ready, ma'am," Jack said quietly. "I'm going to put a shot of bourbon in it for you. Is that okay?"

Mrs. Rothchild nodded. "Yes, Jack. I think I've earned it. Thank you so much."

"I'll take a glass," Clive said. "Minus the hot tea, of course."

Jack smiled. "Of course. One bourbon coming up."

"Can I get by?" Barger's gruff voice sounded behind me.

Garrett and I stepped aside and let Barger pass. He plopped down in a chair, glaring at all of us.

"Ryli," Agent Wilson said behind me, "if you and Garrett could take a seat, please. I'll address everyone at once."

We did as he asked.

"My name is Agent Wilson, and I work for the FBI. My field office is out of Denver. I'm on the train because I was taking a couple days off work to make my way over to the FBI field office in Oklahoma City. When I was made aware of the robbery on the train, I was informed I could not offer my services as an FBI agent. However, with the escalation of a murder, I am now the person in charge. Chief Kimble has been given permission to assist me."

Angelica gasped. "So it's true? Christopher was murdered?"

"Yes," Agent Wilson said. "His body was discovered about fifteen minutes ago."

All eyes turned to me. Once again I wished the floor would open up and swallow me whole. As luck would have it, Jack chose that moment to enter the viewing car carrying the hot tea and bourbon.

"Why would someone murder Christopher?" Clive asked.

"Murdered?" Jack echoed. "I just can't believe it."

"I'm not exactly sure why he was murdered," Agent Wilson said. "But I'd say it has something to do with the stolen diamonds."

Mrs. Rothchild swiped at her eyes. "This makes no sense. Are you saying you think Christopher found out who stole the diamonds and they murdered him to keep him quiet?"

"At this time I'm not sure what has happened," Agent Wilson said.

"Well, what the heck do you know?" Floyd grumbled.

June lifted her hand as though to stop Floyd's words, then slowly lowered her hand. Her eyes looked even more sunk in than the night before. If she'd had a moment's peace, I'd eat my right hand.

"That'll be enough," Agent Wilson said. "Right now Chief Kimble and I are going to secure the crime scene. I'm putting Shirley Jenkins in charge of making sure no one leaves this viewing car."

"Why her?" Harold asked. "I mean, no offense Aunt Shirley, but let's be real right now. What we *do* know is that there is a killer

128

loose on this train, and you want us to trust a little old lady to protect us?"

Aunt Shirley flipped her false teeth out of her mouth, then sucked them back in. I knew she did it for effect, but it was a disgusting habit. "Watch who you're calling old there, sonny."

"Yeah, why her?" Barger demanded. "I'm the one that's head of security on this train!"

Agent Wilson glared at Barger. "Because she's next in line with the most law enforcement experience. And I'm not entirely sure you're totally innocent."

Barger's mouth dropped open, but he didn't argue.

Agent Wilson turned to Aunt Shirley. "Jack is the only one that can leave the room, and that's only to go to the lounge for drinks. Everyone else stays in this room at all times, is that clear?"

"You got it!" Aunt Shirley said gleefully.

"What if we need to use the restroom?" Angelica asked. "What are we supposed to do then?"

Agent Wilson sighed. "We are one hour outside of Oklahoma City. If you cannot wait that long, then Ryli will escort you to the restroom located between the lounge and dining car. Is that clear with everyone?"

A grumble went up in the viewing car.

"Good," Agent Wilson said, obviously not caring that most people didn't like the suggestion. "Now, Mr. Barger, Chief Kimble will take your gun."

Barger hissed. "Why?"

Garrett stood and walked over to Barger.

"Because as the acting law enforcement officer on this train," Agent Wilson said patiently, "I am the only one authorized to have a weapon. You are a suspect in this murder, and as such, you are not to have a weapon. Is that clear enough? Now slowly withdraw the gun and hand it over to Chief Kimble."

Everyone waited with bated breath as Barger did as commanded. Once the gun was in Garrett's hand, Barger flopped back down in his chair.

"Chief Kimble and I will be downstairs if we are needed," Agent Wilson said. "Once the scene has been secured to our satisfaction, we will start taking statements. We have one hour until we reach the station. Hopefully we can put this matter to rest."

Garrett and Agent Wilson descended the stairs, leaving the nine of us alone…ten if you counted Jack. Which I was beginning to think we should.

Harold and Angelica took a seat near the corner and called to Jack to get them a drink. Aunt Shirley motioned me over to where she and Old Man Jenkins were sitting.

"Here's what we need to do," Aunt Shirley said. "We need to solve this case before we reach Oklahoma City. And we need to go over some of our clues."

"Like what?" I asked.

Aunt Shirley pursed her lips. "I'm leaning more toward you being right about Delbert's death. Maybe it was a murder."

I gasped. "Did you find something in Christopher's cabin?" I asked.

Aunt Shirley shook her head. "No. But the two people who have died on this train are both employees. Maybe the theft was just a diversionary tactic."

"Well, then it was a good one, " I said. "This case just keeps getting more and more confusing as we go."

"Which is why your aunt needs to wrap this up," Old Man Jenkins said.

"And how do you propose we do that?" I asked.

Old Man Jenkins smiled slyly. "I'm going to go over and schmooze Barger and buy him a few drinks. Maybe he'll drop me a few clues."

Aunt Shirley looked at me. "And you and I are going to question the others."

Old Man Jenkins got up and stretched before walking away.

"What about Jack?" I asked.

Aunt Shirley frowned. "What about him?"

I sighed and watched as Jack entered the room and handed the drinks to Harold and Angelica. "I hate to say this, but Jack is the last person we know of to have spoken to Christopher. Plus, he was in the lounge the night Mrs. Rothchild asked Delbert about his medication. Jack would have known Delbert took medication. What if we've had this all wrong? What if Jack and Christopher were in cahoots? Right now we aren't sure if Christopher died because he found out who stole the diamonds and he was killed for that information, or if he was somehow involved with stealing the diamonds."

Aunt Shirley frowned. "I suppose that's an angle we have to look at. Okay, keep an eye on Jack, also."

"What are we looking for again?" I asked.

Aunt Shirley grinned. "Reaction. When the time is right, I'm going to pull out my trump card."

"What's that?" I asked.

"I still have the collar of diamonds in my pocket."

I gasped. "Are you serious? You didn't give it to Agent Wilson?"

"Nope. This one is ours to solve." Aunt Shirley patted my knee then stood. "Now, just follow my lead. We're gonna question these people one more time and pick out the thief and murderer before we arrive in Oklahoma City."

CHAPTER 20

I followed Aunt Shirley over to where Clive and Mrs. Rothchild were sitting. Out of the corner of my eye I noticed Old Man Jenkins was inviting himself to sit next to Barger.

"How are you holding up, Mrs. Rothchild?" I asked sincerely.

Mrs. Rothchild shook her head and clutched Muffy tightly to her. "I just don't understand this. I'm so confused. The only thing I can think of is that Christopher discovered who the thief was and when he confronted them...they killed him!"

I saw Clive wince.

"You don't think so?" I asked.

Clive didn't say anything for a few seconds, then patted Mrs. Rothchild on the hand. "Eloise and I have differing views."

"What's your theory?" Aunt Shirley asked.

Clive looked once more at Mrs. Rothchild before speaking. I noticed he didn't let go of Mrs. Rothchild's hand. "I think Christopher was the one that somehow stole the collar. Then someone found out and killed him so that they could keep the diamonds for themselves. Which means that right now, someone in this car has the diamonds on them."

They sure do, but it's not the killer.

"Interesting," Aunt Shirley said as she sat back in the chair. "You know, I hope we can get this cleared up before we get into Oklahoma City. Isn't that where you're getting off to meet with your buyer for the cows?"

Clive's face turned pink. He reached up and adjusted his cowboy hat. "Well, as it so happens, Eloise and I have come to an understanding."

Aunt Shirley lifted her brow. "Really? Do tell."

Clive cleared his throat. "Well, it seems Eloise and I have some feelings for each other. We've decided to hold off on my business in Oklahoma City for the purchase of the cows until we get back to Kansas City."

"What about needing to sell the cows to pay off the huge hospital debt?" I asked.

Mrs. Rothchild slid her hand up Clive's arm. "I know how this must look to you. I'm a good ten years older than Clive. But we're good for each other. Clive can look after me, and I can get him back on his feet without him having to lose his shirt…or his farm. We're gonna be okay."

"Good for you crazy kids!" Aunt Shirley exclaimed. "Let's go, Ryli. Leave these two alone."

Muffy yipped.

"These three alone," I added quickly.

We got up and made our way to the Walshes.

"What do you think?" I whispered.

"I think Clive is in a better position to full-on hook up with Eloise than to just steal her diamonds for a one-time payoff," Aunt Shirley said. "I mean, he admitted he owed a lot of money. The collar—or diamonds really—are valued at thirty-five thousand dollars. He's better off hooking up with her like he is for the long payout."

I crinkled my nose. "That doesn't bother you? I mean, he's basically using her."

"They're using each other. She gets companionship and physical help from someone who obviously likes her. He gets money to pay off his debts and less stress in his life. That's a win-win as far as I'm concerned."

"I suppose."

"Besides, Clive is a large man. He was twice the size of Christopher. He could have snapped that boy's neck in a matter of seconds. He wouldn't need to use a fire extinguisher."

I pursed my lips. "And I don't think Mrs. Rothchild has the strength to lift a fire extinguisher and bash Christopher over the head. Or the demeanor."

"True," Aunt Shirley chuckled. "Let's see what the Walshes have to say."

Angelica and Harold were too busy glaring at each other to notice Aunt Shirley or me.

"So that's really it?" Harold snarled. "You're leaving me because we've hit a roadblock?"

Angelica wiped her eyes. "I can't be poor. I don't know how to do it."

I cleared my throat.

Harold's green eyes flashed at me. "What do you want? Can't you see we're busy?"

"I'm just curious where you've been?" I said. "I mean, I know you had a headache last night, Angelica, but no one has really seen you two since last night around nine."

Angelica narrowed her eyes at me. "What are you implying?"

I shrugged. "I'm just wondering what happened after you left the karaoke party last night."

"We came back to the room. Harold gave me some medication to take, and I fell asleep. It was a migraine, not a headache. Those things put me under."

"And you?" Aunt Shirley asked Harold.

Harold did a little bluster. "I gave Angelica her medication and waited for her to fall asleep before I laid down. I wanted to make sure she was okay."

Aunt Shirley frowned. "So you were up for a while. Did you hear Christopher come back to his room last night?"

"No!" Harold exclaimed. "I'm sure I was asleep by then."

I cocked my head to the side. "And this morning? I don't remember seeing you in the dining car for breakfast. Why's that?"

Harold downed the last of his drink. "If you must know, Angelica and I continued our fight. She has decided she cannot live with a poor man and is divorcing me."

Angelica threw her glass against the wall, shattering it into a thousand pieces. Everyone in the viewing car stopped what they were doing and looked at the Walshes. "Do *not* make me out to be the bad person here, Harold! You're the one that screwed up! You made a slew of bad investments, with not only *our* money, but with our friends' money. I'm just refusing to stay around and help you clean up your mess!"

"Okay," Aunt Shirley said, grabbing my arm. "We can go."

"I'll get that," Jack said as he quickly left Old Man Jenkins and Barger to themselves. "I'll just go get a broom and dust pan."

Aunt Shirley and I made a hasty retreat toward Floyd and June.

"Don't even think of stopping here," Floyd growled as we stopped next to him and June.

June bit her lip. "I'm sure they just want to ask a couple questions." She stuck her hands inside the same gray cardigan she'd worn yesterday and wrapped it tighter around her body. Her pale, gaunt face looked scared.

"We ain't got nothing to say," Floyd snapped. "Keep moving."

June lifted a trembling hand out of her cardigan and tucked a piece of her limp hair behind her ear.

I took a closer look at June. Her eyes were not only sunken in, but they were red and swollen from crying. Her nails were chewed down to the quick, and she looked as though she'd slept in her clothes.

"You okay, June?" I asked casually.

"She's fine," Floyd said.

"I'm fine," June parroted.

"I'm just making sure," I continued. "I haven't seen you in some time."

June looked at Floyd before answering. "I didn't feel like going to the party last night, and I really wasn't hungry this morning."

I nodded my head. "Did you happen to hear anything last night coming from Christopher's room?"

June's eyes filled with tears and she shook her head forcefully. "No. I swear I didn't."

"How the heck would we hear anything down where we are?" Floyd growled. "We're practically at the end!"

A tear slid down June's cheek and she worried her lip back and forth until a tiny drop of blood appeared on her bottom lip. "I swear I don't know anything about what happened to Christopher."

I frowned and thought about what I knew about these two. They were the hardest to read of all the couples on the train. Could Floyd have somehow found out that Christopher stole the diamonds and went in to steal them from Christopher last night? And in Christopher's haste to get away from Floyd, he ran to the bathroom to flush the diamonds down the toilet?

But Floyd is like Clive, he wouldn't need a weapon. I was pretty sure Floyd was used to using his fists as weapons. He, too, could snap Christopher's neck like a twig.

"So why don't you two go on and pester someone else?" Floyd snarled.

June said nothing, just stuck her hands back in the pockets of her gray sweater and huddled down further in the chair.

We left Floyd and June sitting in their misery.

"We've got Barger and Jack left," I said as we strolled over to where Old Man Jenkins and Barger were drinking.

"Bring me another drink," Floyd called out.

"I'm leaning more toward Christopher being in cahoots with either Barger or Jack," Aunt Shirley said.

"Me, too. It's making more sense for the robbery and murder to be centered around the train employees. But I'm still confused as to why Christopher would flush the diamonds."

CHAPTER 21

"Maybe Barger or Jack followed Christopher to his room after the party," Aunt Shirley surmised. "There was a fight as to who would hold on to the diamonds. One thing led to another and Christopher ran to the bathroom to flush the diamonds down the toilet and Jack or Barger came up and smashed in his head."

"Did Jack or Barger come to the door carrying the fire extinguisher?" I asked.

Aunt Shirley shrugged. "Possibly. So maybe that's why Christopher ran to the bathroom to flush the diamonds down the toilet. He knew he was in trouble."

"It's the flushing of the diamonds that has me perplexed. It doesn't make sense. I still think there's an important piece to the puzzle we're missing."

"Agreed," Aunt Shirley said. "Let's go talk to Barger. I don't think there's any reason to talk with Jack."

"Why not?" I asked.

"He's just going to tell us what he told us this morning. He received a text from Christopher around one-thirty stating he was sick and could Jack cover for him. So let's go see what information Barger will spill."

We made the short trip over to where Barger and Old Man Jenkins were sitting nursing their drinks.

"Barger," Aunt Shirley said jovially as she sat down in a chair across the aisle from him. "How's it going?"

Barger scowled and took a drink of whatever liquor he had in his glass. "How do you think it's going? I've been replaced by an old lady."

Aunt Shirley leaned in and laughed like a wild woman. "This old lady could kick your butt in less than ten seconds…then use your lifeless body to wipe up the blood. Remember that."

I bit my lip to keep from laughing. Old Man Jenkins beamed at Aunt Shirley.

Aunt Shirley slapped her hands down on her knees. "So, let's start again. How ya doing, Barger?"

"Fine," Barger gritted between clenched teeth.

"Good to hear," Aunt Shirley said. "So tell me what happened last night after you left the party?"

"Can I give anyone a refill?" Jack asked as he stopped in front of us.

Old Man Jenkins and Barger both shook their heads.

"There's nothing to tell," Barger said. "The party ended around midnight. I went back to my room and fell asleep."

Jack frowned. "Actually, I think I saw you after one."

My eyebrows shot up and I sent Aunt Shirley a look.

Her only response was a tiny smile.

"What?" Barger demanded. "No you didn't."

"Yeah," Jack said. "We pulled into Albuquerque around one. I could have sworn I saw you walking through the train during that time."

"I can assure you that you didn't see me," Barger argued.

Who is telling the truth?

Aunt Shirley caught my eye and gave me a small nod.

Without warning she stood up and whistled. "Can I have everyone's attention, please?"

The viewing room grew quiet as all eyes were on Aunt Shirley.

"I think I forgot to tell everyone the good news!" Aunt Shirley exclaimed.

"There's good news?" Mrs. Rothchild asked.

"There sure is," Aunt Shirley said, taking in the faces all around her. I followed suit, telling myself to watch for the reaction that wasn't natural.

"I forgot to tell you all I found the collar with the diamonds!" Aunt Shirley reached into her polyester pocket and yanked out the metal chain with the blue leather band holding six pink diamonds.

A collective gasp went up…then pandemonium and chaos.

"How can this be?" Mrs. Rothchild demanded.

"Well I'll be danged!" Clive shouted. "This is great!"

"Does this mean Christopher didn't steal them?" Mrs. Rothchild asked.

"If you found them," Harold said, "how do we know who the killer is?"

"I bet you had them the whole time," Floyd said, pointing a finger at Aunt Shirley. "You're probably the thief *and* the killer."

"Give them to me," Barger demanded. "As the train's security personnel, I should be in charge of keeping them safe."

"I'm not sure I'd trust him," Jack said, narrowing his eyes at Barger.

More shouts and accusations arose.

So much so that Garrett and Agent Wilson slowly emerged from downstairs.

Garrett took one look at the chaos and shook his head at me. A slow grin spread over his face as he saddled up next to me. "I have to say, this took longer than I thought."

I frowned at him. "What do you mean?"

Garrett wrapped his arm around me. "I figured Aunt Shirley would be up here doing her thing and having people up in arms and pointing fingers in a matter of minutes."

My mouth dropped open. "That's a horrible thing to assume."

Garrett shrugged. "It worked, didn't it?"

I giggled then instantly sobered.

"What's wrong?" Garrett asked.

"I know who killed Christopher."

Garrett's eyes grew wide. "You do?"

"Yeah," I sniffed as tears filled my eyes. "I looked for the reaction that didn't make sense. And it's the last person I thought would kill someone."

CHAPTER 22

"June," Garrett said gently. "Why don't you come with us?"

"How did you know?" June whispered as she slowly rose from her chair and wrapped her cardigan around her small frame.

"Know what?" Floyd bellowed as he stood up from his chair. "What the heck is going on here?"

I marched over to where Floyd was now standing and planted my finger in his chest. "You're gonna want to sit down and shut up. June is going with us."

"Why? She don't know nothing." He took another drink out of his glass. "She never has."

A whistling sound reverberated on my left side and Floyd Hughes let out a scream that sent me reeling backward.

Sticking out of Floyd's chair was a ninja star!

"Oh my goodness!" Aunt Shirley cried in exaggerated shock before anyone else could react. "Where did that ninja star come from?"

"Shirley Jenkins!" Garrett bellowed, turning to glare at Aunt Shirley.

Aunt Shirley blinked innocently at Garrett. "What?"

"You crazy old bat!" Floyd yelled. "You're gonna—"

In a flash, Aunt Shirley dug out another ninja star from her bra. Angelica let out a scream and slid off her chair onto the floor of the train.

"You're gonna want to watch yourself," Aunt Shirley said to Floyd. "Or this next one might just hit ya. I've been practicing my aim since the last time I had to use these."

"What—how?" I shook my head. "How did you get these on the train?" I shook my head again. "No, wait. How are you carrying ninja stars on your body without cutting yourself?"

Aunt Shirley shrugged. "I'm pretty amazing, kid. When are you gonna learn that?"

Agent Wilson strode over to Floyd and proceeded to cuff him.

"What are you doing?" Floyd demanded. "You can't arrest me. Arrest that crazy old woman for attempted murder!"

"She was defending the life of her niece," Agent Wilson said calmly. "Now, the two of you are going to calm down until we get this cleared up."

June wiped the tears from her cheeks and looked at Aunt Shirley. "I still don't understand. How do you have the diamonds?"

"What have you done?" Floyd demanded.

"I stole the diamonds!" June said frantically. "Or at least I thought I did."

"What?" Floyd roared. "Why would you do that?"

"Why?" June screamed, her face suddenly bright red. "Why?" She leaned back onto Garrett, lifted her leg in the air, and gave Floyd a nice little kick to a certain part of his anatomy.

The man dropped like a sack of flour.

"Can't say he didn't deserve it," Garrett murmured.

"The why is easy," June raged at Floyd, who was rolling around on the ground groaning in pain. "I wanted away from you. I hate you! You're a horrible, evil man! I saw my chance to

144

escape…my chance at freedom…and I took it!" June suddenly stilled, as though the fight had completely left her. "Or at least I thought I did."

"But why kill Christopher?" I asked.

June started sobbing again. "I didn't. I swear to you I didn't. I don't understand what's going on. I'm so confused."

"How did you know she was the killer?" Mrs. Rothchild asked me.

"Because when Aunt Shirley produced the diamond collar, June looked shocked and reached down to pat her cardigan pocket. Her reaction didn't match everyone else's."

"Wait. Why does Aunt Shirley have the collar?" Garrett demanded.

Ut oh!

Aunt Shirley waved the collar we found in the air. "I may have forgotten to tell you that Ryli and I found the diamond collar when we found Christopher's body. Totally slipped my mind, Ace. Honest mistake."

Garrett's nostrils flared and a tic appeared in his jaw.

"Then what do you have?" Garrett asked June.

June reached down in her pocket and handed Garrett six tiny diamonds that looked like they'd been cut out of a leather collar.

"My diamonds!" Mrs. Rothchild cried. "Thank you for finding them!"

"Wait," Clive said. "If June has the diamonds, how does Shirley also have the diamonds?"

"I still say as the security officer on this train I should be the one to secure the diamonds," Barger argued.

Garrett gave him a death glare.

"Yes, why are there two sets of diamonds?" Mrs. Rothchild asked. "Muffy only had one."

"Good question," Agent Wilson said. "I'll take all the diamonds. Garrett, you bring June downstairs, and we'll get this settled."

Garrett led a weeping June down the stairs.

"What about me?" Floyd groaned from his position on the floor. "When can I be released?"

Agent Wilson and Garrett continued down the stairs as if they hadn't heard him. I smiled at Aunt Shirley and together we walked over to where Mrs. Rothchild and Clive were sitting, leaving Floyd to manage on his own.

"Well, I guess that's that," Clive said.

"But why did she kill Christopher?" Mrs. Rothchild asked.

And what about Delbert? How did he fit into this? Was his death really a result from a heart attack or stroke?

I sighed. "I guess that's what Garrett and Agent Wilson will have to figure out." I glanced down at Clive's watch. "We're less than thirty minutes to Oklahoma City. That will give them plenty of time to figure out why she killed Christopher."

"Who wants another drink?" Jack asked from the lounge door.

"I do," I said. "I could use a nice, strong margarita right about now."

"You got it."

He strode through the doors, past Angelica who was now off the floor and back to sitting rigidly in her chair. Her arms were crossed over her chest and she was staring out the window. Harold looked just as miserable.

"I need to use the restroom," Barger said.

"Can't you wait twenty minutes until we reach the train station?" Aunt Shirley asked.

"No. I need to go now."

I sighed. "I'll take him. I can pick up my drink from Jack while I'm back there."

I followed Barger through the door and into the lounge. Jack was behind the counter hacking away at the ice and mixing my drink.

"Hey, Ryli. I'm about finished with your drink." Jack said as he stabbed the pick into the block of ice again. "What are you two doing back here?"

"Barger here needs to use the restroom," I said.

Jack pointed to the restroom by the entry of the dining car. "It's open."

"You heard him," I said to Barger. "I'll wait right here."

Barger huffed and started for the bathroom. He took one step before pivoting and pushing me so hard I flew into the barstools.

"What the heck!" Jack exclaimed. He ran around the counter to help me up, but before he could reach me, Barger grabbed me by my ponytail and yanked me to him, my back pressed against Barger's chest.

"Stop where you are," Barger said. He lifted his foot and withdrew a knife from his boot.

I blinked in surprise. "Well, crap."

Barger laughed. "Crap is right. Your stupid husband and that worthless FBI agent didn't do their jobs and frisk me."

"Why should they have?" I asked. "You were supposed to be the good guy."

Jack took a step toward us, and Barger lifted the knife to my throat. "Nope. Not gonna happen. What *is* going to happen is you're going to go downstairs and tell *Chief Kimble* that if he wants to see his wife alive again, he's going to hand over those diamonds. The real ones. Trust me, I know the difference. I'm the one that made the fake set."

Jack cut his eyes to me.

I nodded the best I could. "Do as he says, Jack."

Jack blinked at me then cut his eyes to the bar then looked back at me.

I furrowed my brow. I had no idea what Jack was trying to say.

"Go on!" Barger roared. "You have five minutes to get the real diamonds and get back up here." He yanked my head back and I groaned. He ran the knife over my cheek and I screamed in pain.

Jack turned and fled out the lounge door.

CHAPTER 23

"Why?" I asked.

"Why did I kill Christopher?"

"And Delbert. You killed Delbert, too, didn't you?"

Barger laughed. "I did. That little pipsqueak, Delbert, overheard Christopher and me going over the plan one last time as we were pulling into the Kansas City train station. I had no doubt he was going to blab the minute he got the chance to."

"How did you do it?" I asked, my eyes scanning the counter, trying to figure out what Jack had been trying to tell me before he left.

"While he was still working the dinner shift, I sneaked into his room and took a handful of his blood pressure capsule and opened them up. I then dumped out the powder, found Christopher in the kitchen, and had Christopher put the powder in Delbert's water. The porters all drink water during the dinner rush to keep hydrated. I knew it would hit Delbert's bloodstream instantly and make him lethargic and woozie, giving me an advantage later on when I attacked him."

"I remember he was staggering and looked pretty awful when he came into the lounge to say goodnight to us all," I said.

"Then when he retired to his sleeping car, I made sure to give him plenty of time to take a couple more pills. See, Delbert would think he wasn't feeling well because he hadn't taken his pills. By the time I knocked on his door, he was too doped up to fight me. I subdued him, opened the rest of the pills and put them in a nice stiff alcoholic drink—which he should never drink while taking the medication—and fed him the rest of the pills."

Well, what do you know? My instincts were right.

"So Christopher was in on it the whole time?" I asked.

"Yep. And it was the perfect plan. If you really want to know who's to blame for your imminent death, blame the old, rich lady upstairs. She didn't follow any of her normal routines."

"Mrs. Rothchild? What do you mean?" I tried not to panic as I felt blood sliding down my cheek.

"That woman has been riding this train for the last year faithfully. Her habits are well known. After breakfast she would retreat back to her cabin to nap. Every single time. So, Christopher and I get the idea to rob her. Once she had retreated to her room after breakfast, he would slip inside her car and exchange the collar. Muffy loved Christopher. She'd never bark at him. Mrs. Rothchild would never know."

Barger suddenly growled, picked me up, and threw me onto the floor. I was totally unprepared for the move and rolled into the barstools. "Only this time...the old lady doesn't go straight to her room after breakfast. Want to know why? Because she's decided she wants to stay in the viewing car and wait for you and your husband."

I grabbed hold of the top rung of a barstool and tried to pull myself up. I swiped my shoulder across my cut cheek.

"So that stupid idiot Christopher decided to improvise," Barger went on, yelling behind me. "He decided to try and swap the collar while Rothchild was sleeping in the viewing car that first morning."

I shook my head to clear it. "That morning when Garrett and I caught you and Christopher leaning over Mrs. Rothchild?"

Barger grabbed hold of my hair once again and hoisted me up to face him. "Yes. He was about to swap out the collars when you walked up and asked what was going on."

"But something must have happened for you to kill Christopher?" I squeaked.

Barger let out a barking laugh. "Christopher and I had been searching nonstop for the stolen diamonds all day. We figured one of you must have seen the same opportunity we'd seen and snatched them before we could, not even bothering to hide the theft by replacing a fake collar. By the time the karaoke party was in full swing, and we still hadn't found them, Christopher said he was going to get rid of the fake necklace because it was too risky to have it in his possession."

"So you were actually searching for the real diamond collar to keep for yourself and exchange with the fake collar when you searched everyone's cabins the morning of the theft?"

"Yes. I figured I could catch the thief, be the hero, and swap the collars before anyone knew."

"But Christopher put a kink in your plan when you still hadn't found the real necklace by that evening," I said.

"He was afraid he'd be caught with the fake diamond collar and someone would think it was the real one. I was still sure we could figure out who stole the real diamonds and get them back. But Christopher wanted nothing to do with it. I told him I'd meet him in his room around one-thirty to talk—after the party but before people started loading the train in Albuquerque. When he opened the door and saw me with the fire extinguisher, he must have known my intention. He took off for the bathroom, grabbed the fake collar off the counter, and flushed it down the toilet. Or at least I thought he did, until I saw your stupid aunt yank the collar out of her pocket declaring she'd found the real diamonds."

I almost laughed at the image of Aunt Shirley brandishing her treasure for everyone to see. It had been pretty humorous. She honestly thought she'd found the real diamonds.

"So, after I killed Christopher, I took his phone and texted Jack, pretending to be Christopher, hoping to skew the time of death."

"You're crazy," I whispered. "But smart."

"Let go of my wife," Garrett said from the doorway.

I tried to move my head to see him, but Barger once again had a firm grip on my hair.

"Now why would I want to do that?" Barger sneered.

"Because how else are you going to get the diamonds?" Garrett asked.

"Don't!" I cried. "Don't give them to him."

"Shut up!" Barger yelled.

He pushed me away from him and slapped me across the face. I reeled back and fell onto the counter...and my eyes landed on what Jack had been trying to tell me.

I screamed again and flung my arms across the counter even more. I figured I was over playing my hand, but I didn't know what else to do.

"Let her go, Barger," Garrett said. "You don't need her. I have the diamonds. Take me if you want a hostage."

My hand latched onto the ice pick at the same time Barger grabbed hold of my hair again. At this rate, I was going to be bald.

He yanked me up from the bar by my hair and held me against his chest. I cradled the ice pick in my hand against my own chest, hoping to hide the weapon.

"This is how it's going to play out," Barger rasped against my ear. "You're going to give me the diamonds. I'm going to take your lovely wife with me until we reach the outskirts of town. When I think it's safe, I'll let her go."

"Don't believe him!" I cried. "He's crazy! Not only did he kill Christopher, but he killed Delbert, too!"

"Shut up!" Barger hissed.

Garrett reached inside his pocket and withdrew the diamonds not encased in the collar. "Here are the real diamonds. Let's talk this out."

"There's nothing to talk out," Barger said as he ran the knife down my chest. I simultaneously lowered my hand to my stomach so he wouldn't feel the ice pick I had stashed in my own hand. "One false move and your wife will take a knife to the heart."

The heck I will, Barger! This is my honeymoon...I'm not dying on my honeymoon!

"Set the diamonds on the table and back up," Barger demanded.

Garrett's eyes never left mine as he moved toward a table and set the six diamonds down on the table.

"Back up," Barger demanded.

Garrett slowly stepped backward toward the door, his arms raised in surrender.

"Pick them up," Barger demanded in my ear.

He dropped his arm from across my chest, but still had ahold of my hair. I could move forward just enough to pick the diamonds up off the table with my left hand. The diamonds weighed next to nothing.

"We should be pulling into the station at Oklahoma City any minute now," Barger said. "You have my word. Once I get out of the city, you can collect your wife."

I rolled my eyes. "Don't believe a word he says. He already told me he was going to kill me."

"Shut up!" Barger said as he yanked my head back onto his shoulder.

I chose that moment to make my move. Raising my right hand, I thrust backward with all the force I had and stabbed Barger with the ice pick.

He screamed and released my hair. I whirled around to face him, ready to finish him off if I had to. A screaming Barger reached down and tried to pull the ice pick out of his stomach. At the same time, Garrett ran full force and tackled Barger, both men falling to the floor.

The lounge door flew open and Agent Wilson ran in, gun drawn. He glanced at Garrett, who was busy yanking the pick out of a screaming Barger and handcuffing him behind his back.

"You okay?" Agent Wilson asked me as he holstered his weapon.

I nodded my head. I could still hear Barger's screams of pain rattling around in my brain as I buried my head in Agent Wilson's chest.

"You got everything under control?" Aunt Shirley asked.

I lifted my head off Agent Wilson's chest and started to full on ugly cry.

"Give her to me," Aunt Shirley said. "I'm the only one that can handle her when she's like this."

It was on the tip of my tongue to curse at her...but I couldn't find it in me to do. Instead, I wrapped my arms around Aunt Shirley and wept.

CHAPTER 24

After Barger had been hauled away by the police, I gave the diamonds to Agent Wilson for safekeeping, and Aunt Shirley had handed over the plastic baggie of extra powder we found in Delbert's cabin, I finally settled down and stopped blubbering…and remembered the cut.

"How bad is it?" I gently ran my hand down my cheek. I could still feel the sting from the blade, even though the blood had been wiped away from my tears.

"Stop worrying about it," Garrett said. "It doesn't matter. We'll have the EMTs look at it soon."

I looked at Aunt Shirley. "Tell me the truth."

Aunt Shirley broke eye contact with me and looked over at Old Man Jenkins.

My hand covered my mouth and I began to sob. I knew if Aunt Shirley couldn't tell me the truth…it was bad.

"Stop," Garrett said as he gathered me in his arms. He brushed back the hair from my face. "You are Ryli Jo Sinclair-Kimble. Strong, independent, and beautiful. You are not defined by one portion of your body."

I rested my forehead on his chest. "It must really be bad if you have to give a speech like that."

He let out a sharp laugh. "I'm not gonna lie. You're probably going to have a small scar."

I cried even harder.

"Stop," Garrett begged. "This isn't the end of the world. Besides, you should be happy. You caught the bad guy."

"And got a scar to show for it," I whined.

He lifted my head and looked at me, wiggling his brows. "I think it's sexy."

I spit-laughed at him as I wiped the tears from my eyes. "What the heck does that even mean?"

He knocked away my hands and gathered my face in his palms. "It means I think you are the most beautiful woman I've ever seen. It doesn't matter to me if you have a little scar on your cheek. That's not who you are." He leaned down and gently brushed his lips across my cheek. "Or maybe it is. Maybe the rough, fierce type is exactly who you are."

I sucked in a ragged breath and hiccupped. "I want to go home. I want my mom."

"I know," Garrett cooed. "But the police are here and they need to take your statement."

"We'll be with you every step of the way," Aunt Shirley assured me. "By the way, good call on Delbert's death. Even though I suspected, you got Barger to confess."

"With all the excitement after the diamonds were stolen," Garrett said, "no one really thought much about Delbert's death and if there was a connection. After all, he'd died before the diamonds were stolen."

The next hour crawled by at a snail's pace. I answered all the questions the police threw at me. A couple of them were impressed with my backward stab and congratulated me on a job well done. However, I still had to spend the night in the hospital once the x-rays came back. When Barger threw me into the barstools, he bruised a few of my ribs. That, combined with the stiches I needed for my cheek, ended up as an overnight. I balked the whole time, wanting nothing more than to go home to my mom. Garrett was a trooper and assured me he understood my need for my mom. I fell asleep crying in his arms.

***

"How're you feeling, Mrs. Kimble?" the nurse asked when I opened one eye.

"Okay," I croaked.

"Good to hear," she said. "You have company."

I opened the other eye. Garrett was holding my hand and smiling at me. "Hey, there. Glad to see you're back with us."

I gave him a watery smile. "I feel better. I guess I was just tired from talking with the police and crying so much."

He leaned down and softly kissed my hurt cheek.

"So! Did you get a story?"

I looked over to my left and groaned.

"Hank!" I exclaimed. "What are you doing here? And can't you think of anything else besides your next story?"

"No," Hank said. "I expect a story on my desk in two days!"

Mindy tsked at her husband. "Hank, give the girl a break. Can't you see she's sore and trying to recover."

"Hey, baby!"

"Mom!" I looked over my right shoulder and saw my mom, Doc Powell, and Matt huddled almost behind my bed.

"We wanted to surprise you." Mom wrapped me around her and I breathed in her scent. I'd missed her more than I ever thought I could.

"I love you, baby girl," Mom cooed.

"I love you, Mom."

"What about the rest of us?" Matt asked as he lifted his phone up in the air. "I got Paige on FaceTime. She insists the twins are begging to see their Aunt Ryli."

"They are," Paige insisted from inside the phone.

I sat back in my bed and took in the people around me. Mom, Doc Powell, Matt, Garrett, Aunt Shirley, Old Man Jenkins, Hank, Mindy, Paige via the phone, and even Clive and Mrs. Rothchild were huddled around my bed.

"What are you all doing here?" I asked.

"We couldn't just let you suffer alone," Mrs. Rothchild said. "Clive and I decided to get off the train and stay a couple days with his friends so that we could be near you when you finally came to."

"And when Garrett called and told us what had happened," Mom added, "we all banded together and rode down here to bring you home."

"I'm just sorry I'm missing out," Paige hollered from the phone.

My eyes filled with tears. "Thank you. It means the world to me."

Garrett leaned down and kissed my head. "Everyone in this room loves you, Ryli. Don't you ever forget that."

"When can I go home?" I asked.

"The doctor should release you sometime today," Mom said.

"Until then," Hank said, "you're stuck with our company."

I looked at the people packed in my hospital room and my heart felt full. "I don't mind."

"Eloise, you need to tell Ryli about June," Aunt Shirley said.

Mrs. Rothchild stepped forward and laid her hand on mine. "When I heard why June had stolen the diamonds, my heart broke for her. The police are insisting they have to prosecute her for the theft, but I've already hired her a great attorney. Hopefully she'll just get probation when everyone realizes why she did it and how even I am standing up for her."

Clive smiled lovingly at Mrs. Rothchild. "Eloise has even offered to let her move in with us at her house in Kansas City until June can get on her feet again."

"Yes," Mrs. Rothchild agreed. "My house is plenty big enough."

Tears filled my eyes. "I'm so glad. I hated the thought of June rotting away in a jail cell, even though it meant she wouldn't have to be with her husband."

Aunt Shirley nodded. "But hopefully now she can put her past behind her and move on with her life. A life without an abusive husband keeping her down."

***

I broke free from the hospital around lunch time. I was sitting in the wheelchair they make you ride out in, waiting for my ride to pull up to get me, when I heard a familiar sound.

"You brought the Falcon!" I exclaimed.

"Thank goodness!" Aunt Shirley cried. "I was wondering how we were all going to get home."

Matt pulled the Falcon over to the curb and jumped out.

"Hank and I drove it down for you," Matt said to me. "You won't be able to drive, but at least you can ride in style."

I stepped out of the wheelchair and gave Matt a big hug. "You're the best big brother a girl could ask for."

"I'll drive!" Aunt Shirley said as she made a grab for the driver's side door.

"*I'll* drive," Garrett corrected her.

Aunt Shirley looked at me and grinned. "Can't blame me for trying!"

I laughed and walked over to the passenger side door, running my hands over the Falcon. Her beautiful turquoise finish glistened in the cool November air. I was willing to give up the controls to Garrett as long as it meant I could still be a part of her. I plopped down in the seat, leaned my head back, and knew I was home.

CHAPTER 25

"Where are we going?" I asked Garrett as he led me blindfolded down a street.

We'd been back home in Granville for a few days, and things were back to normal. I wrote Hank the story he was wanting, recounting what had happened on the train and my near-death experience at the end. The twins looked like they'd grown four months instead of four days, and I vowed never again to let one day go by without seeing them. I didn't want to miss out on anything.

"It's just a little bit farther up here," Garrett assured me.

I was due to take my PI test in five days, and I was a ball of nerves. I needed to pass the first time...not because I wanted my license, but because I wanted Aunt Shirley to stop grilling me at every waking moment.

"We're here," Garrett said quietly.

"Where's here?" I asked. "Can I take off my blindfold now?"

I felt Garrett's arms wrap around me as he kissed the top of my head. "I'll do it. But before I do, I just want you to know how much I love you. I'm always amazed after one of your little stunts just how much I can worry."

"Your speech started out so good," I grumbled.

Garrett chuckled in my ear. "Anyway, as I was saying, I'm always amazed after one of your little stunts how much I love you...and how much I worry about you. But the time has come for you to spread your wings, Ryli Jo Kimble. And I know that. There've been a lot of changes in your life recently. Your mom starting a new relationship, Matt and Paige getting married, Aunt Shirley getting married, our wedding, the twins being born, the disastrous honeymoon—which I'm totally blaming Aunt Shirley for—and I know how much you've wrestled with getting your PI license and starting a new chapter there. So, I thought maybe I could do something to ease a little bit of your anxiety."

I gasped. "What have you done? Can I lift the blindfold now?"

Garrett grasped the edges of the blindfold and slowly lifted it off my face.

I was standing in front of an abandoned storefront off the main drag downtown. Right around the corner from Legends Salon and Nails.

"Okay," I said slowly. "We're in front of what used to be Myrtle's Five and Dime store when I was a kid. Nothing's been in here since then. What's going on?"

Garrett thrust his arm out in front of his body, a key dangling from his fingers. "What's going on is that this is yours. I bought this building for you so you and Aunt Shirley had a place to go when you start getting work."

I staggered backward. "Are you serious?"

He turned and stared at me. "Yeah. I am. I wanted to give you your own space...but still make it close to me. In case I needed to keep an eye on you two."

I laughed. "Garrett, I can't believe you did this. How long have you been planning this?"

"Pretty much since you admitted to me you wanted to get your license a while back. I figured I'd better be proactive or who knew where you two would end up having an office."

I laughed and took in the building again.

My building.

Numerous bricks had crumbled over the years and were missing from the facade, and the windows were so filthy I couldn't see inside. Which was probably a good thing, because I had no idea what was growing or crawling around in there. It would take weeks to clean…and even then, it would probably still be disgusting.

But it was mine!

I jumped up and down like a madwoman and threw my arms around Garrett. I gave him four or five quick kisses on his neck.

"You like it then?" he chuckled.

"I *love* it!"

I glanced over my shoulder when I heard the loud creak of the wooden screen door. Standing inside the filthy building was Aunt Shirley, Old Man Jenkins, and Mom. They were all shaking their heads and grinning at my display of affection.

"How long have you guys been inside?" I asked.

"Long enough to know this place will probably never get cleaned," Aunt Shirley said.

"Nonsense," Mom argued. "It just needs a little elbow grease and it will be perfect."

I snickered at her optimism and walked inside my new office.

The lights were on, but the fixtures were so coated with dust you could barely tell. The smell was a cross between a dank cellar and dirt. The cement floor was caked with dust, dead bugs, and other unidentifiable objects. But it was a gigantic room, probably forty-eight by forty-eight. I could make out a small door in the back and remembered that used to be the bathroom.

But the best part of the space was the wide, wooden staircase off to the side that led up to a second-floor loft. That was where Myrtle always kept her office. I figured that's where we could meet clients and maintain some privacy for them.

"I think Aunt Shirley and I can make a go of it here," I said. "Don't you, Aunt Shirley?"

I saw the glint of excitement in her eyes as she took in everything. She could downplay it all she wanted, everyone in the room knew she was ecstatic.

"I mean, it's gonna take a lot of work," Aunt Shirley said slowly. "I'm probably gonna be putting in long hours just to get this place up and running."

"That's a shame," Old Man Jenkins deadpanned.

I giggled.

Aunt Shirley gave him her evil eye. "But I think once we get everything cleaned up and organized," she turned to me and grinned, "it's gonna be a nice space for us to do some damage."

"There's something else," Garrett said.

"More?" I asked. "What *else* could there be?"

Garrett pointed to a narrow door about ten feet from the start of the wooden staircase. "That door right there. It's not a closet. It's actually a staircase that leads to an apartment upstairs."

I gasped. "I have an apartment upstairs?"

Then I cringed thinking about what that must look like. How many critters were calling that place Home Sweet Home.

Garrett shrugged. "Who knows. Maybe someday you'll get so big you need to take on an employee and they'll need a place to live."

Images of what I could truly make of this place floated through my head and I almost staggered from it all. This was my time. My time to try and make something of myself. I'd always felt suffocated by the mundaneness of my small-town life. But now I had a chance to really have a career. To do more than just go to Hank's office and write fluff pieces for people to read. I had a chance to really make my mark in life.

"It's perfect," I said. "In fact, it's more than perfect." I turned to Garrett, tears falling from my eyes. "It's the most amazing thing anyone has ever done for me."

He wiped the tears away with his thumbs. "I knew you'd appreciate the beauty once you saw it." He kissed the tip of my nose. "I love you. And you deserve a chance to make this dream of yours come true."

I laughed through my tears. "You're praying to God I fall flat on my face and give this dream up, aren't you?"

Garrett threw back his head and laughed. "Maybe a little."

I turned to survey my space again. This was my baby now, and there was no way I was going to give it up. No matter how many times I fell on my face. And it would be a given I'd fall…probably more times than I could count.

But I'd have Aunt Shirley there with me every step of the way to pick me up, brush me off, tell me what a complete failure I was at my job, and shove me back into the fire. And I'd love every minute of it.

Look out world, here I come.

Ryli Kimble, PI.

Next Stop Murder

ABOUT THE AUTHOR

Jenna writes in the genre of cozy/women's literature. Her humorous characters and stories revolve around over-the-top family members, creative murders, and there's always a positive element of the military in her stories. Jenna currently lives in Missouri with her fiancé, step-daughter, Nova Scotia duck tolling retriever dog, Brownie, and her tuxedo-cat, Whiskey. She is a former court reporter turned educator turned full-time writer. She has a Master's degree in Special Education, and an Education Specialist degree in Curriculum and Instruction. She also spent twelve years in full-time ministry.

When she's not writing, Jenna likes to attend beer and wine tastings, go antiquing, visit craft festivals, and spend time with her family and friends. You can friend request her on Facebook under Jenna St. James, and she has a blog http://jennastjames.blogspot.com/. You can also e-mail her at authorjennastjames@gmail.com.

Jenna writes both the Ryli Sinclair Mystery and the Sullivan Sisters Mystery. You can purchase these books at http://amazon.com/author/jennastjames. Thank you for taking the time to read Jenna St. James' books. If you enjoy her books, please leave a review on Amazon, Goodreads, or any other social media outlet.

24258737R00093

Made in the USA
Columbia, SC
25 August 2018